BEST OF THE

Winning and Shortlisted Stories

2025

Edited by Ed Bicioc & Amanda Scotland

NOT QUITE WRITE PRESS

First published in 2025 by Not Quite Write Press

Not Quite Write Press
ABN 85 157 104 734
PO Box 9067
Wyoming NSW 2250
Australia
notquitewrite.com

The stories within this anthology are works of fiction. All names, characters, businesses, places, events and incidents in this book are either the product of the author's imagination or used in a fictitious manner. Any resemblance to actual persons, living or dead, or actual events is purely coincidental.

© Copyright in the individual works remains with the authors 2025
© Copyright typesetting, cover and internal design Not Quite Write 2025

A catalogue record for this book is available from the National Library of Australia

Best of the Not Quite Write Prize for Flash Fiction 2025: Winning and Shortlisted Stories

ISBN 978-1-7637165-2-0 (paperback)
ISBN 978-1-7637165-3-7 (eBook)

Edited by Ed Bicioc and Amanda Scotland (non-Australian English spellings retained)
Internal design by Amanda Scotland
Cover illustration and design by Vanessa Browne, Vee Creative

Write on!

— Ed & Amanda

CONTENTS

Foreword

What an incredible year 2025 has been for *Not Quite Write*.

No sooner had the ink dried on our first print anthology than we began preparing for the launch of our new *FLESH Fiction* erotica competition, quite appropriately, on Valentine's Day. We were overjoyed at the response we received, and we cannot wait to unleash the winning stories on the world in book and podcast form in 2026.

In June, we returned for our third year running to the *Words on The Waves Writers Festival*, where we had the opportunity to interview writers, poets and journalists including Nikki Gemmell, Maxine Beneba Clarke and Blanche D'Alpuget, as well as soak in author talks and events. (All our interviews are available on the *Not Quite Write Interviews* podcast stream).

In October, we released our one hundredth episode and celebrated our third anniversary as a podcast, and it was wonderful to receive so many messages from listeners and entrants celebrating along with us. Recording that episode was a positive reminder of how far we've come as a podcast, and of the wonderful community we've gathered along the way. We've watched in amazement as our episode downloads and listener numbers have bloomed. It's staggering to imagine our voices resonating in so many eardrums.

But throughout the year, our cornerstone has remained the *Not Quite Write Prize for Flash Fiction*. The book you currently hold in your hands (or that is held by the RAM of your eBook reader) represents the very best stories from 2025, along with additional commentary from the authors and judges. These are stories that range from comedy to drama, highbrow to low. For every *Adolescence*, there is a commensurate measure of 'eye-children' and 'vajankles', and we are supremely proud of each and every one. We feel an incredible affinity towards our entrants, as well as gratitude for having found our little niche on the Internet.

But this anthology also marks the end of an era. The anti-prompt has officially been retired, to be replaced with the *Write-Off*, our exciting new prompt format starting in 2026. The send-off has been bittersweet. The anti-prompt has inspired thousands of amazing stories, with creative twists on writing rules that never would have come into existence without it. But we are confident that the *Write-Off*, with its emphasis on competitiveness and fun, will encourage our entrants to write what most speaks to them, and truly let their freak flags fly!

We hope you'll join us again.

— Ed

Introduction

About the Not Quite Write Prize

Now closing out its third year, the *Not Quite Write Prize for Flash Fiction* has cemented its place as a fixture on the international short fiction competition circuit.

In 2025, the competition again challenged writers around the world to craft compelling stories of up to 500 words in response to a set of three prompts:

Word prompt: Entrants were given a word that they had to use somewhere in the main body of their entry. The word could be included within a longer word provided the original spelling was retained.

Action prompt: Entrants were given an action, which they had to feature somewhere in the main body of their entry. The action could occur before the beginning of their story or after it ended provided it was referenced either directly or by clear implication within the main body of the entry or its title.

Anti-prompt: The infamous anti-prompt challenged entrants to break a traditionally accepted 'rule' of writing. More information about the anti-prompt can be found on page xiii.

The shortlisted stories in this anthology earned their authors cash prizes, and in the case of each winning author, a trophy.

While the competition has earned a reputation for showcasing what some might affectionately call 'lowbrow' comedy, it's just as likely to reward 'highbrow' literary fiction, with each shortlist—and by extension this anthology— boasting a broad spectrum of narrative genres and styles.

The *Not Quite Write Prize* is celebrated for its transparent judging process, with its judges delivering dramatised readings of the winning and shortlisted entries along with deep insights and extensive global feedback via the *Not Quite Write Podcast* and website.

Not Quite Write Daredevils take it a step further, volunteering to have their entries dissected by judges, Ed and Amanda, on-air. The Daredevil episodes of the podcast have become fan favourites, pairing a dramatic reading of each story with a balanced yet refreshingly unfiltered discussion of its strengths and weaknesses.

This anthology represents the anti-prompt's swan song, with an exciting new prompt format promised for 2026 and beyond.

WTF is an anti-prompt?

Like many writing competitions, the *Not Quite Write Prize* uses creative writing prompts to inspire and challenge entrants. Between 2023 and 2025, it also included something called an *anti-prompt*. The anti-prompt challenged entrants to break a traditionally accepted 'rule' of writing while still telling a great story.

The art of writing is a no-holds-barred creative pursuit which will look different for everyone. The craft of writing, however, is subject to many helpful precepts which can guide writers to elevate their prose. These are what we call the writing 'rules'. Understanding these rules can help writers craft more compelling stories.

By challenging entrants to break a writing rule, we were not issuing a license to ignore the rule and its reason for existing. Instead, we were challenging them to think about why the rule exists, to recognise how it works to elevate prose, and then find a creative way to break the rule without breaking their story.

In this anthology, you will observe some of the many creative ways our authors have approached the following anti-prompts:

Break the rule, 'Write what you know.' (January 2025)
Break the rule, 'Kill your darlings.' (April 2025)
Break the rule, 'Use active voice.' (July 2025)
Break the rule, 'Show, don't tell.' (October 2025)

About the judges

Ed

Ed embraced the virtues of a short attention span long before TikTok made it cool. He's penned the opening lines of dozens of unwritten novels and written hundreds of popular short-form reviews on Goodreads. But it wasn't until he discovered flash fiction that he truly found his niche. Ed has earned his place on the *Furious Fiction* longlist and showcase multiple times with vulgar classics like *A Spoonful of Sugar* and *Who Shat Their Pants?* These are achievements of which Ed is both proud and deeply, deeply ashamed.

Today, like most writers, Ed prefers to procrastinate rather than write. Fortunately, he's bitten off way more than he can chew with the *Not Quite Write Podcast* and *Not Quite Write Prize for Flash Fiction*, though he still likes to sneak in the occasional flash (or *FLESH*) fiction entry when the mood strikes him.

Amanda

A storyteller all her life, Amanda first ventured into flash in 2021, seeking an accessible path to creativity after a tragic family event left her critically time and energy-poor.

She struck gold on her third attempt: winning the Australian Writers' Centre's *Furious Fiction*. Since then, she's longlisted in a range of flash and micro fiction contests, earning publication for her 'weird suburban' short fiction in *Ellipsis Zine* and *Nightmare Fuel*.

These days, Amanda spends her time channelling her writing passion through the top 10-ranked *Not Quite Write Podcast*, and *Not Quite Write Prize for Flash Fiction*.

Despite swearing black and blue (but mostly blue) she would NOT enter any writing competitions in 2025, Amanda inevitably snuck a few into her calendar.

Once a wannabe contest goblin...

Dean

Dean Koorey is a professional copywriter, co-creator of the *Furious Fiction* flash fiction competition and a frequent writer of short fiction.

His accolades to date include winning the 2023 *New York City Midnight* 250-word story competition, winning 2nd place in the 1000-word *Writing Battle*, shortlisting twice in the 2024 *Not Quite Write Prize for Flash Fiction*, as well as podium finishes in many other competitions.

In 2025, he began guest judging for the *Not Quite Write Prize* (thus sadly ending his quest for the pointiest trophy in all the land), and he loves finding stories with creative takes on prompts and strong narrative voices.

His coffee order is an oat milk flat white, or macadamia milk if you've got it.

JANUARY

2025

Overview

The January 2025 *Not Quite Write Prize for Flash Fiction* challenged writers to create an original piece of fiction of no more than 500 words, which:

included the word **RING**.

included the action **'opening a door'**.

broke the writing rule, **'Write what you know.'**

The competition drew **346** entries from authors in a reported **19** countries around the world. That's **167,170** words for our judges to read. That's about the same number of words as ***The Shining*** by **Stephen King**.

Please enjoy the following top six stories from this round of the competition...

YOU'LL NEVER SEE THIS COMING

Isabelle Berns

The last face Paul saw was that of his daughter.

Smiling.

Glowing.

Broken.

Within arm's reach.

Still no telling where his attention went.

Where it *had* been?

Probably nowhere.

Everywhere.

Funnelled.

Scattered around the globe.

Calendars.

Inboxes.

Stocks.

Breaking news.

Rage-bait.

Repeating reels.

Doom scrolling first thing on a Monday morning, last thing on a Monday evening, and on every day ending in 'y'.

Where his attention went?

Probably nowhere.

More so by the second.

Certainly not the sodden street, or the press of commuters, backpacked and coffeed up.

In Paul's final moments, the world might have revealed itself anew. No longer boxed into those empty morsels of replayed novelty curated to his taste.

Starved from the feed that saturated but could never satiate, his ravenous eyes might have found something of substance, had he just looked up.

Something tangible.

Something solid.

Something four-wheeled and roaring into a green phase.

He hadn't. That was the crux of the matter.

Paul might have recognized the woman sketching portraits outside his usual cafe. The busker eager to catch his attention. He might have seen the skyscrapers around Hamilius Station, staring from windowed heights, clouds swiping by overhead. He might have heard the chorus of klaxons trumpeting in the newest casualty. Screeching brakes heralding his demise as he stepped into the road.

Even now, he might have noticed oily rainbows shimmering past, carrying the dust of the city off the edges of the world, through a whorly grate, and into the unknown.

Paul might have known his friends unedited.

His ex's mind unfiltered.

His own opinions unsponsored.

He might have witnessed Katie's first steps unlooped.

Unique.

Precious.

Never to be repeated by the tip of a finger.

Could he register the bus doors opening? The figures swooping in around him? See the checkmarked messengers composing short-form testaments? Recording his end from behind the murky, pearly-fogged glass of the 11 Bus to Walfer?

Did he notice thousands of black eyes witnessing his incomplete crossing for the world abroad? Carrying his broken body cloudward post-haste, hastily posted via the very medium he had followed into this mess?

Had he lived, he might have crossed himself on a stranger's screen. Recognized himself among the real-time chaos of rush hour. A man at a junction. Between could and should, want and have. A forced perspective. A mind rammed back into a body of flesh and hair, windshield-studded, limbs splayed. Spreading a feathered red halo on the wet street with each slowing breath.

His phone holding him warmly by the hand – its gaze never faltering, barely even flickering – the last face Paul saw, was that of his daughter. Smiling, cracked, from behind a screen she shared with a clock that would run on without him. His Katie. On the very distant fringes of his frayed consciousness. Where he must have kept her far too often. Hundreds of miles away. The image of her right there at his fingertips, with 5% to go on the battery.

About the author

Isabelle is a Luxembourg-based writer with a soft spot for descriptions and fun facts. She loves books, films, plays and video games alike, provided they get her mind traveling with sufficient leg space.

Author's insights

'*You'll Never See This Coming* stems from a valiant attempt at a daily habit tracker, a warm phone battery, and reading up on thousand-eyed angels (the original messengers before there were apps for that sort of thing). The initial image that got the story rolling, was that of multiple eyes or cameras locking in on a shocking event before reporting it to the world abroad.

'The central questions of the story became: if we were asked to pass review on our lives, summing up years spent eating, sleeping, working, could we actually account for the hours spent on our smart devices? And what would it take for a person to break free of something that has such a phenomenal hold on them?'

Ed's comments

Isabelle has chosen a narrative voice that perfectly embodies her major theme—that of disconnectedness and inattention. The fragments scroll past like a social media feed, distracting us until reality hits.

What drew us to this story was its relatability and its relevance to our time. As readers, we see our own face reflected in Paul's cracked screen and ponder what it is that we, too, fail to experience each day as we are captivated by our phones' irresistible glow.

Amanda's comments

From the first moment I encountered this story, I knew there was something special about it.

I remember commenting on social media during the judging process that the author had taken a big risk, but that I believed it had paid off. The risk I was referring to was Isabelle's choice to deploy these staccato-like sentence fragments. Although unconventional, they worked perfectly to mimic that fragmented feeling we experience when we doomscroll.

There's power in taking risks. True, it doesn't always pay off as marvellously as it has for Isabelle on this occasion, but in my opinion this risk-taking is vital to creativity. It's about taking the universal and making it personal; in this case, taking a shared fear about our overreliance on screens and pushing it to its logical extreme. Fiction allows us to really *go there*. Doing so in a uniquely individual way is what connects the reader and the author on a deeper level.

The circularity of this story (the 'end in the beginning' and vice versa) cemented it as a satisfying, albeit disquieting, reading experience.

It's a story that makes you look up and marvel at the clouds... even if just for a moment.

THE TASTE OF PI

Alexandria Bellani

The first time I hear her laugh of golden Fibonacci spirals, I know I have to meet her. Big parties are too much colour, noise, and flavour, but I'll brave this one a few minutes longer just to learn her name.

Anna.

It doesn't suit her, I blurt, with her plaid miniskirt and starless midnight eyes. 'Anna' tastes like cold canned peas.

Her friends are outraged, but she throws her head back and laughs in golden ratio, and I forget that any other algorithm has ever existed. She says her full name is Anastasia—what does *that* taste like?

I roll the syllables on my tongue, testing every letter. The salty 'A's' and sweet 'S's'. The savoury 'N' and spiced 'T'. 'I' is my least favourite vowel—so tart and overbearing—but in her name, it softens like butter.

Brown sugar, I answer, and pi. I don't clarify 'the number' because at least 'pie' is a flavour normal people can imagine.

She leads me 'round the room, introducing me to everyone and asking what each name tastes like. I don't mind performing party tricks, with her hand in mine.

Over hours, I tell her 'Caroline' tastes of old lemonade, 'Chase' of plums, and 'Sasha' of ice scraped off the inside of a freezer. She tells me she's a jazz musician and that she loves artists. She winks, saying I must be one, to have an imagination like this.

I don't know how to say, 'I'm not' and 'I don't.' That, even now, I'm running the numbers on our chances, and she's too beautiful, and I'm too weird. This doesn't end with 'happily ever after'. I spare my heart and slip out while she's getting us drinks.

She finds me at work a week later. I startle when she slams open my office door with a victorious 'ah-ha!' cracking the air with gold lightning.

Coffee flies out of my 'freak in the spreadsheets' mug as I throw my arms wide to cover the whiteboard of partial derivatives at my back. As if I can stop her from seeing how poorly suited we are, as if it matters after I ran away.

She doesn't look at the whiteboard, though, when she calls me an asshole. The word is a platform-booted kick to the sternum. She says she's never been ditched before and needs to know what happened.

She wants answers.

The only kind I'm good at is numbers.

So, I write up the odds of two people finding each other. Falling in love. Staying in love. Especially someone like *me*. Someone who knows the numbers on the whiteboard are written in blue marker but sees rainbows. Someone who approached the girl with the golden laugh and told her that her name tasted like peas.

Blue marker squeaks out lavender threes, navy eights, and crimson zeroes before her hand halts mine.

'Run these numbers,' she whispers.

Then she kisses me, and it's music, and sugar, and pi, and gold—

And flawless Fibonacci spirals.

About the author

Alexandria Bellani is an aspiring novelist living in Canberra, Australia with her husband, kids, and dogs. She enjoys food, puns, and making people cry. When she's not at her day job, she moonlights as a certified Contest Goblin. Alexandria's work also appears in Elegant Literature's *Fearsome Folklore* and *Crossroads and Consequence* issues.

Author's insights

'I'm primarily a speculative fiction writer, so when I saw the anti-prompt, I celebrated for about an hour. Then I thought about what "write what you know" really means and spent the rest of my weekend staring at a word document and going insane.

'This idea came from playing with the concept of inventing colours. I fell down a research rabbit hole that ended with reading pages and pages of poetry by artists with synaesthesia. I knew I wanted to explore it through a character, but I wasn't sure of the story. I wrote about four thousand words of different ideas, going through a dozen characters and plots, including one particularly yuck piece about a cannibalistic serial killer. Thankfully, I came to my senses when I realised there was one thing I know even less about than psychopathy: *math*.'

Ed's comments

This story is the embodiment of 'Poe's Single Effect'. The protagonist's synaesthesia and love for patterns are presented not simply as personality quirks, but as the cornerstone of character development and the lens through which we as readers can understand and connect with them.

Alexandria submits all elements of her narrative to this single frame, filling her story with colourful, multisensory images that feel like falling in love.

Amanda's comments

I was instantly moved by this gorgeous story, and much like the Fibonacci sequence it references, its impact only grows with each subsequent reading.

We often talk on the *Not Quite Write Podcast* about the difficulty of delivering compelling genre fiction in the flash format, but this romance stands apart through its rich character development and delightfully divergent voice.

There's a lyrical quality to the writing, so the story unfolds almost like a song, inviting invites readers to experience the world through this character's unique, synaesthetic perspective. As a result, the story becomes as much about empathy as it is about love, and as much about our relationship to other people as it is about the relationship of these two characters to each other.

I had the pleasure of meeting Alexandria at my *Start Writing Flash Fiction* workshop for Central Coast Libraries, and I've since enjoyed getting better acquainted with her and her writing through the Daredevil experience. I'm convinced she's only just begun to scratch the surface of her talents, and I can't wait to see what other hidden gems she unearths!

RULE OF THUMB

Elise Scott

Nothing swells a man's ribs with hope like the sight of a shiny brass doorknob and a deed that says it's his. There's no elation to match that first time he pushes his key into the waiting lock and feels the slow, sure yielding of its tumblers.

Mine was a real beauty, made in the French style by craftsmen up in Ames. Perfect for the door Grampa carved when he was my age. He worked these acres his whole life. Now it was my turn.

I scooped Elodie up in my arms and shouldered open the door. The hinges sang of squealing children, of calling sooey into the sunrise, of the whistle and hoot of Monday night football.

'Welcome home.' I let the words fall into her hair as I lay her down on the bare floor.

The good honest smell of paint and sweat and pine varnish muted her lilac perfume. Here began my new life as head of the family. Here, I'd be happy.

'Travis, I—'

I put a finger over her peach-sweet lips. 'Hush.'

This was a moment to savor. I unwrapped her slowly, marveling at how fragile she was. I would protect her. Cherish her. I would not be like my father.

And Elodie wouldn't be like Ma. She wouldn't flash a fuchsia lipstick grin and show my cum-stained sheets to my friends as they devoured her cinnamon rolls. She wouldn't rub herself like a cat in heat while she gazed at her community college students. She wouldn't cheat. Wouldn't leave.

As I moved over Elodie, she flushed pretty as a berry dipped in cream, her elegance mussed but undiminished by my hungry touch. I tried to think of other things, to slow myself down, but it was over too soon, and I wasn't gentle.

Her porcelain hand pushed at my chest, her dainty golden ring vanishing into my thick bear's pelt. Like my father, always the coarse and massive beast.

Until I found him in a room empty as this one, cloaked in the smells of paint and sweat and pine varnish. The crags of his silhouette had been freshly broken by the avalanche of his grief.

'You heed your Grampa's Rule of Thumb, son. Someday, you'll find yourself a sweet young wife. You be sure and scuff her up a bit. If you let 'em stay too shiny, eventually they'll leave.'

His hollow eyes fixed on Ma's newlywed smile behind cracked glass. He curled his paw closed around her. 'I didn't listen. Don't be like me.'

So, when Elodie cupped my face, dark eyes vulnerable as a winter doe, I pushed her away.

I pushed hard.

Afterward, of course, I apologized. I always apologized. 'Don't know my own strength.' I'd spoon cherry pie between her trembling lips. Or Maker's Mark.

Truth is, I always knew the way my hands would wear the brass off that gleaming French doorknob little by little, revealing the chipped and bitter nickel underneath.

That's what made it mine.

About the author

Elise Scott writes from their lived experiences of queerness, disability, neurodivergence, fat-positivity, and petting three cats with two hands. Their life has been an adventure, from facilitating equine therapy for trauma survivors to counseling at-risk youth with the aid of an inordinately large sub-woofer and beyond. They earned their BA from Mount Holyoke and their MS from Capella University.

Their debut novel, described as a cozy mystery featuring three kittens with the ability to bend the laws of physics, who must solve a murder to save their rescuer from the human pound, is forthcoming from *Crooked Lane* in May 2026. Their short work has appeared in *The Advocate*, *Choices: An Anthology of Reproductive Horror*, *The B'K*, *Five Minutes*, *Chaotic Merge*, *Knee Brace*, *HerStry*, *All Existing*, and *Quibble*, among others.

Find out what they're working on now at elise-scott.com.

Author's insights

'Credit for inspiring this story has to go to Ed and Amanda. The anti-prompt 'write what you know' led me (like most of the writers who participated the competition, I bet) to ask what is most unknowable. As a survivor of spouse abuse, one of the first questions that rose to my mind is how an abuser could treat someone they purportedly love with such cruelty.

Yet we're all human. We're complex and broken and luminous and lost and lovely, each and every one of us. We're seekers. So, I challenged myself to gaze into the darkness until my eyes adjusted, searching for nuance. Writing this story was deeply cathartic for me. It helped me understand how acceptance remakes grief into something easier to carry.'

Ed's comments

Elise wrote this story as an attempt to inhabit the mind of someone they couldn't understand—an abuser. What an amazing and brave take on the anti-prompt!

I love the metaphor or the doorknob (also a great take on the action prompt), and the exploration of the influences of family culture on abuse.

A powerful and chilling story.

Amanda's comments

It takes a lot for me to mark a story as a favourite on first read, but this one took that title.

For a start, it's incredibly well-crafted, with the sexualised and persistent metaphor of the doorknob delivering satisfying cohesion from the first word to the last. More than that, it's the deep emotional resonance offered by the insight into the mind of 'the villain' which leaves a lingering impact long after the final word.

Intimate partner violence is a theme we see crop up time and again in the competition. At times, it's invoked for dramatic impact, and at other times (like this one) it's delivered from a place of deep personal truth. It's this truth that connects reader and author, even if only briefly, through time and space. This is the essence and beauty of great art.

I feel very fortunate to have since become better acquainted with Elise, who generously devoted countless hours as a guest judge on our erotic flash fiction competition, the *Not Quite Write Prize for FLESH Fiction*. I have found Elise to be an incredibly kind, generous and wickedly funny person, and I wish them every success in their writing career.

CHATROOM_523

E. C. Heath

Margo's quilt muzzles the notification's whine.

user9837213, 1:21 a.m.

u rly have a dick?

ttgxrl444, 1:25 a.m.

Yeah

user9837213, 1:25 a.m.

hard to believe. ur so beautiful

She considers telling him it isn't *so* far-fetched for a beautiful girl to have a dick. Decides against it.

user9837213, 1:27 a.m.

i've got one too

attachment: IMG.9330.jpeg

It's no work of art. An imagined Seba conducts critique, dissecting its composition ('the subject's asymmetric curve'), rapping on her square glasses as if to refocus the picture, frizzy hair bobbing like an independent body. She dubbed Margo's last piece *unruly. Recalcitrant.* Margo supposes her teacher might label the grainy image dusting her headboard with blue light *evocative*, but of what she can't verbalize.

What did Seba say two classes ago about Ezra's work, the one of condom wrappers? *Unbeautiful.* Yes, that's it.

user9837213, 1:29 a.m.

u wanna come over n have some fun?

The cat sitting on the stoop is statue-still, collarless. She hopes it isn't his, or at least, if it is, he'll keep it outside. Climbing the steps, sweeping right, steering clear. Yellow eyes tracking.

user9837213's place is a shadowy thing sprouting from the snow-guttered sidewalk. No moon out tonight, what kind of omen is that? Such superstitious-speak reminds her of yesterday's horoscope: *your big transition will soon end.* She laughs all over again, her real laugh, sort of husky, not the affected bleat donned around classmates. Around Ezra.

Margo finds the doorbell and a note (she looks closer, it's the reverse of an envelope) crudely taped to the adjacent siding. DO NOT RING, it reads, in blocky, fat-tipped Sharpie. She obeys, knocks thrice. Unzips her coat. An owl cries.

The door opens, unexpectedly quiet. From what Margo can make out, he isn't unattractive. She typically enjoys guys like this. Tolerates them, at least, these used-car men, stubbled, scruffy, with decent mileage despite the dented doors. But she can tell now. The cat is his. He has that same look in his eyes, even worse when he smiles. Like he knows something she doesn't.

user9837213, 3:42 a.m.

had fun 2nite. we shld do it again sometime

Margo opens three different social media apps despite not consciously wanting to. Muscle memory. She's training herself to stop clicking on them, she read an article about it — or, okay, watched a video — but the impulse is always irresistible during these stretches, this yet-to-feel-whole-again stage. She switches to the camera instead, a practice the article (video) recommended. Self-reconnection, or something.

Her reflection is murky, a mosaic of pixels the color of beer bottles. Smudged mascara, purpling neck. A voice crowing in the back of her mind: *poor thing*. She snaps a picture, not exactly knowing why. Maybe she can use it for something, submit it to Seba for critique. What would Ezra think?

Unbeautiful, she remembers, repeating it to herself, letting the word erode a smooth canyon through her memory, one she can traverse until she's through the dormitory doors.

ttgxrl444, 8:51 a.m.

Sure.

About the author

E. C. (or just Evan) Heath is a student at Brown University working towards a degree in the Literary Arts (probably — he hasn't declared his major yet). He is grateful to *Not Quite Write* for advertising on Instagram, or else he probably wouldn't have found their podcast and competition, signed up on the final day sign-ups were open, written his first ever piece of flash fiction, and been featured in this anthology. He also must uphold a promise and shout out his good friend Isabel Levine, who proofread his entry (while sick!) and suggested the deletion of two words, which he thinks was probably what got him into the shortlist.

Author's insights

'I found Margo pretty early on in the writing process and quickly became attached to her as a character. I probably could have tested out some other ideas before banking it all on her, but I don't really tend to write that way — and it all worked out in the end! I'd been tossing around ideas for a story with a trans protagonist before I'd even heard of this competition, and the anti-prompt for this round was eventually what pushed me to try and see what I could come up with.

'In the end, though some of Margo's experiences are ones I will never share, I think her intense desire for validation is something that, at least to some degree, is universally relevant. Though Margo doesn't really overcome this desire, I think I found the energy, or heat, of this piece within that lack of character growth. Sitting with Margo, staying stagnant alongside her at this point in her life, was what I found to be the most truthful, compelling, and resonant — and when it comes to writing what you don't know, that's kind of all you can look for.'

Ed's comments

What I loved about this piece is its complexity and ambiguity. It doesn't present us with a simple narrative story arc. It's more of a character study that explores a host of issues that young people have to deal with, like peer acceptance, image and the search for oneself.

The narrative is gritty, unsanitised, and feels very current. Though we only get a slice of Margo's life, I feel immersed in her complex world filled with omens, casual sex, and a search for connection.

The ending is ambiguous, but strangely satisfying. As in life, the voyage of self-discovery is never complete, however we are somehow left with the feeling that Margo can handle what life throws at her, and that she will be okay.

Amanda's comments

This story drips with subtext, artfully 'showing', without needing to spell it out, that Margo is a trans woman, and this rendezvous is laced with shame for both parties.

The insight into Margo's direct thoughts invites empathy for her self-destructive choices. Through Margo's unique perspective, we confront that universal suspicion that we ourselves must also be *unbeautiful* (perhaps, more precisely, *unlovable*).

Evan's choice to cut to black instead of depicting what we can only infer was violent sex, perfectly encapsulates Margo's dissociative state. It invites readers to similarly check out at the lover's doorstep and only check back in once Margo has safely returned home. This is what we refer to as emotional resonance, where the story captures a feeling in such a way that the reader can not only understand the characters' emotional perspective, but *feel* the emotion with them.

Now *that* is beautiful.

LOVE IN THE TIME OF FLATULENCE

Greg Schmidt

I slump into my car and fart—a ripping release from another day of moronic managers and meandering meetings. And another day I didn't bloody talk to him. For weeks I have been trying to find the courage to ask Jason out, to woo him with some perfect piece of conversation.

In the lunchroom today, I had my chance.

'Hi Ellie,' he said to me, stirring his tea.

Our eyes met, and my confidence evaporated. My voice went with it and all I could manage was a mumbled, 'Hey.'

An awkward pause followed, punctuated by the ting-ting of his spoon against the cup. Unable to fill the void, I just left.

Now, I start the car to leave this day behind, when there's a tap at the window. It's Jason, making a motion for me to wind it down. I do so; nervous and excited.

It's exactly then that the results of my earlier gaseous emission arise, and a horrid stench hits my nostrils. Jason leans in closer and opens his mouth to speak. I'm mortified and quickly try to raise the window, but I'm too late. His lips curl, and his face twists, as the odious odour wafts through the half-open window to greet him head-on. He coughs and holds the back of his hand to his mouth.

'Oh, God,' I sputter. 'I'm sorry,'

'It's—' he begins, but I panic and close the window, sealing me in with my dread creation. I speed out of there, leaving him just a vision in the rear-view.

The next day passes and I manage to avoid Jason at work. What would I say to him, anyway? Any mystery—any allure—will have dissipated with the lingering foulness of a fart to the face.

I breathe a sigh of relief when I enter the lift to leave. But as the doors close, someone darts between them to join me; Jason, as fate would have it. I shuffle my feet and stare down at my phone. The awkwardness from the lunchroom yesterday surrounds us again and we do not speak as the lift descends.

Suddenly the silence is shattered by the unmistakable trumpeting of a fart. It ends with an upturned squeak, as if posing a question. When I look to the source, Jason is grinning at me.

'So Ellie,' he says, as if nothing had escaped his arse a few seconds prior. 'You wanna grab a drink after work sometime?'

I'm equal parts embarrassed and dumbfounded. 'Did... did you just ask me out by farting on me?'

He raises an eyebrow. 'You started it.'

It's a fair point, and I can't stifle a chuckle that comes from within.

'Is that a yes?' he asks.

I'd been so worried about the perfect way to ask him out, but perhaps it never needed to be perfect. In response, I cock my hip and let out the tiniest toot. We laugh, and when the lift doors open, we step out into the fresh air together.

About the author

Greg Schmidt came late to the writing game but is attempting to make up for lost time by writing as much as his procrastinating nature allows. His somewhat similarly themed story, *Untitled #2*, featured in the *Best of the Not Quite Write Prize 2023-2024*. Not all his stories feature bodily functions, but the published percentage is rather high.

Greg's work features twice in this anthology. You can find his other contribution on page 101.

Author's insights

'It's not based on a true story, if that's what you're wondering. I'd written a version of the scene in the car previous to the competition, but I'd never been able to make anything of it other than a silly joke. For my take on the anti-prompt, I challenged myself to write in an unfamiliar genre, being romance, and that scene struck me as the ultimate awkward moment in any burgeoning love affair. With that as a starting point, I tried to create a story that kept the lowbrow comedy, but at its heart remained a genuine romance.'

Ed's comments

This is Greg's second toilet-themed entry, and the second one to make the *Not Quite Write Prize for Flash Fiction* shortlist (I'm not sure what that says about us as judges!)

Nonetheless, this story hooks the reader from the opening line, and delivers a fully-fledged rom-com storyline, complete with meet-cute, conflict and a happy ending. Not bad for only 500 words!

Amanda's comments

My initial comments on this story read, 'Hahahahaha. Hilarious. No notes.' But I suppose I should elaborate here...

This is *not* just a silly story: it is an incredibly well-crafted flash rom-com, with a satisfying structure others would do well to imitate.

Aside from including the necessary conflict and 'all is lost' moment, another trick Greg has employed here is to make the character's weakness the key that unlocks their luck in love. In Alexandria Bellani's story (on page 26), it was the character's neurodivergent worldview. Here, it's the farting.

I smiled throughout this story and laughed out loud at the 'upturned squeak'. I love it when authors bring their playful side to this competition, and even more so when they deliver on the craft, too.

VISITING YOU, ONE YEAR LATER

Kris Schnebelen

I imagine your alarm waking you, a shrill buzz rattling your walls and clawing your eardrums. Or maybe you've changed it to something more serene, like birds tweeting against a gentle river's flow. Or maybe there is no alarm anymore.

You're sitting up, arms stretching to the sky, every vertebra in your spine popping up your back, taking turns. You're grabbing your phone, checking your email, mostly filled with spam from all the online stores you've shopped. Maybe you've unsubscribed from those emails. Maybe you don't grab your phone. Maybe you don't get out of bed.

You're moving into the kitchen, a fresh cup of dark roast coffee with a pinch of sugar the way you start your day. Maybe you started using cream. Maybe you drink blonde roast, black. Maybe you drink tea now. Maybe you don't go to the kitchen first at all, instead starting your morning with a shower. Maybe you don't have a ritual anymore. Maybe you're still in bed.

It's your day off, so you're wearing something casual. An oversized Coldplay T-shirt—your favorite band. Maybe you wear tank-tops now, or oversized sweaters. Maybe your favorite band is something different. The Strokes, Gorillaz, Poolside. Maybe you listen to country now. Pop. Electronica. Maybe it isn't your day off. Maybe you have a different job. Maybe you have no job. Maybe you're still in bed.

You're fingering through your jewelry. You choose the ring I proposed to you with, the one white-gold band set with a fourteen-karat diamond. Maybe it's the ruby one your grandmother gave you. Maybe it's a different one I don't know of. Maybe you have more rings than I remember. Maybe you sold them all. Maybe you're still in bed.

You're doing that thing you've always done, where you stare in the mirror and squish your unruly hair, draw your hand around your waist, stare at the length of your neck. There is no one there to tell you that you look beautiful. Maybe there is, and they're holding you now as they whisper what I used to into your ear. Maybe there isn't, and you dwell on the little things that never mattered. Maybe you're still in bed.

You're hearing the doorbell ring. You're considering what to do. Is it your mom? Jehovah's witness? Me? Is it worth answering? Should you pretend you're not home? Maybe you're not home. Maybe you're still in bed.

I'm ringing your doorbell. I've been standing for an hour, wondering if I should even be there. I've bitten my cuticles clean off, the edges of my nails red and raw. My ears are burning. No matter how much I focus on my breathing, the air can't keep in my lungs. I've memorized every smudge and every piece of scuff on your welcome mat. It's the only thing I'm sure about you anymore.

I'm hoping you're still in bed.

You're not.

You're opening the door.

About the author

Kris Schnebelen (they/them) is a writer from Texas with a BA in English Literature who works as a clerk at their local library. They have short works featured in several publications and are currently working on their debut fantasy novel.

Author's insights

'I fretted about the anti-prompt 'write what you know' because the concept is ultimately paradoxical—once I write what I don't know, it becomes something I know. So, I instead approached it in a sense of 'write what is simultaneously known and unknown,' which is a concept that can be understood, one many people know very well from simply existing in the world. One example of this is lost relationships and friendships: you know a version of a person from one point in time, but that version of them may or may not exist anymore. You simultaneously know and don't know them, and that Schrödinger's effect remains until you reconnect, if ever.

'This led to me creating a story in which this effect takes the forefront. The main character visits someone they've once had a relationship with and once knew intimately. But this relationship was broken, and time has passed. Will this person be the same as they remember? Or have they changed into someone unrecognizable? This second entity is unknown, and yet known far too well as the main character can recall intimate traits contrasted to what they could've become. This is an answer kept from the reader, as it ends before the two characters can interact again, the door opening representing that shattered effect. That's the point of no return, where the unknown becomes known.'

Ed's comments

What a great example of a story that successfully breaks the rules. We often say that specificity through carefully selected details is the key to creating rounded characters. In place of specificity, *Visiting You, One Year Later* presents us with a string of 'maybes.' We also warn against excessive internality, yet the action of this story takes place almost entirely in the protagonist's imagination.

In this case, however, the ambiguous descriptions serve to amplify the inner tension and uncertainty felt by the protagonist, and perfectly capture an emotional state which we have all felt at one time or another in our lives. There are also several concrete details, like the T-shirt and the engagement ring, which help us paint a picture of these characters and who they might have been to each other earlier in their lives.

Similarly, the internality is less noticeable here, because the protagonist's imaginings are very much active and present. They are not reminiscing about the past or exploring abstract feelings, they are describing actions that are taking place (albeit theoretically) in the here and now.

We here at *Not Quite Write* believe that rules are made to be broken. But doing so in a competition setting can be a risky game. Well done, Kris, for successfully walking this line.

Amanda's comments

This story delivered satisfying cadence, providing structure for the protagonist's meandering internal monologue. Through it, Kris also delivered an intriguing take on the anti-prompt, exploring what it means to know a partner intimately for a time, only to find them completely unknowable after the relationship ends.

While I would normally advise against a cliffhanger in flash fiction, in this story the cliffhanger perfectly mirrors the protagonist's emotional state, allowing us as readers to share the anxiety of what might come next for this former couple.

In life, not everything is tied up with a nice little bow, and in fiction, I can't help but hope for a second chance for this risk-taking ex-fiancé.

JANUARY 2025 LONGLIST

The following list represents the remaining longlisted entries, in no particular order:

- **WILDCARD WINNER** – MR CLARENCE'S SECRET GARDEN by Philippa Freegard
- THE SELKIE WIFE by Tabbie Hunt
- TEMPORAL THRESHOLDS by MM Schreier
- DOVE COTTAGE by Chloe Paige
- YOU DO THE MATH by Deidra Lovegren
- SHELDON THE SNAIL BLAZED A TRAIL by Erin Brandt Filliter
- TO THE DJ WHO INSISTS ON PLAYING *OUR HOUSE* EVERY MORNING AT 9:00 A.M. by Sally Reiser Simon
- A SLOW PASSAGE by Luke Melvin
- MYSTERY by Emily Rinkema
- 547.5 DAYS by Sophie Thompson
- GOING UNDER by Christina Wilson
- IBS – INTENSE BATHROOM SCENE by Jack Lewis-Edney

- LOCKED IN WITH NO WAY OUT by Kerry Goldsworthy
- RED DOOR by KT Downs

The following story did not make the longlist but received a wildcard prize:

- **WILDCARD WINNER** – MOUSEFUCKER by R.C. Barajas

Note: Each judge has awarded a wildcard prize to an entry which did not make the shortlist but which we otherwise felt deserved recognition.

APRIL 2025

Overview

The April 2025 *Not Quite Write Prize for Flash Fiction* challenged writers to create an original piece of fiction of no more than 500 words, which:

included the word **SEAL**.

included the action **'wiping out'**.

broke the writing rule, **'Kill your darlings.'**

The competition drew **307 entries** from authors in a reported **12 countries** around the world. That's **150,103** words for our judges to read. That's about the same number of words as ***Salem's Lot* by Stephen King**.

In this round, we called on the expert judging assistance of our friend and *Furious Fiction* co-creator, Dean Koorey, for the first time.

Please enjoy the following top six stories from this round of the competition...

ZOMBIE BABE

Louise Walton

I can't blast her. Not my Jenny-babe, even with her eyes crazy as a roll-on deodorant ball and that textbook zombie swagger. I mean, it's kind of sexy, really. I lower my blowtorch.

Dead leaves scrape as she drags a foot forward.

The constable next to me squeaks. 'Ah... Stop!... O-or I'll shoot!' Can't remember his name—pen-pushing nerd from the Nulkaba side office—but with the Plague wiping out half the police force, we've got jittery amateurs like him on field patrol, aiming his blowtorch about as steady as the windsock on Mooney Mooney bridge. But he'll still get Jen if he presses the trigger. They're proper blowtorches, not those ones from Bunnings you get for crème brûlées or clearing the dunny air after a steamer—I'm talking Hollywood flame-throwers.

Jen pauses, wavering on the spot.

Our radios crackle. *'Kill the damn zombie! What are you waiting for?'*

My rookie mate answers. 'The Plagued One has... has halted. Over.'

We aren't meant to call them zombies. Some high-up wanker decided it's not people-focused language. I half get the point now that it's my girlfriend, but 'Plagued One' is sort of a turn off. Whereas 'Hot Zombie Babe'... well, that's got a ring to it, putrefying flesh or not.

I nudge Rookie. 'She looks harmless, right?' Maybe I can convince him not to fire.

Maybe me and Jen can run away into the Watagans and survive off the land, and she'll be my Wilson, only I'll be Steven Seagal instead of Tom Hanks, because I'm more Navy SEAL material. Well, less navy, more seal, but I reckon I'd be close if I did push ups.

Rookie lowers his weapon. 'Yeah, she... she seems harmless.'

For a second, Jen's blank eyes flicker with that old spark I remember, when I'd lie there smoking, with her tucked up beside me playing with my chest hair. She'd gaze up at me and say, 'It's only one chest hair, babe, maybe you should just pluck it.' But I never did, because I loved the way she twirled it while telling me I was *her* one-and-only.

'Jo-shu-a?' she moans.

That's not my name. But Rookie's voice shakes like he just watched the end of Red Dog. 'Jen?'

I turn to him. 'You know her?'

He ignores me, stepping towards her. 'Hey, Jenny-babe. Let's go, we'll run for the mountains. We'll be like Jane and Tarzan, only I'll be Sylvester Stallone instead of Brendan Fraser.'

She nods at him, cheating slobber-lips groaning, and forms a love heart with her fingers, except two are missing so it looks like a damn moustache, which Joshua has, and I don't. So, she wants more bristle on her gristle?

I reach down my shirt and wrench out my one and only chest strand, shoving it into the end of my torch barrel. I raise my flame-thrower, ignoring Joshua's arm still in range, aiming level at her festering, clawed moustache-heart.

I can't blast *my* zombie babe. But I'll blast someone else's.

About the author

Louise Walton lives on NSW's mid-north coast with her husband and three children (and chickens, rabbits and a dog). She loves wordplay, comedy and Aussie dramedy. She started writing for fun a few years ago when she read a boring novel and thought she could do better. She couldn't. But she might one day.

Besides *Not Quite Write*, she has had winning stories in *Writing Battle* and *New York City Midnight*, and was a finalist in *Australia's Best Yarn 2024*.

Author's insights

'I'm usually writing for international judges (senses of humour undetermined) so I can't tell you how liberating it was knowing my words would be read by three very amusing local critics. Plus, they said NOT to kill my (literary) darlings— surely that was code for "write a simple plot then ramble in introspective Aussie for as long as I want"? My process was PURE STUPID ENJOYMENT.

'It was also one of those dream writes where every ridiculous thought led to the next: 'wiping out' > zombie apocalypse > zombie 'darling' > sleazy chest hair scene > ambiguous 'chest hair'—many or one? > hair envy > 'seal' prompt = grotesque cohesion! I'll let the reader decide if it's genius or just someone who never matured past Year 9, I'm sure there'll be some mixed opinions...

'P.S. I apologise for the gristle line.'

Ed's comments

Comedy often does well in the *Not Quite Write Prize for Flash Fiction*, but this one was a cut above.

From the wonderful images of roll-on deodorant eyes and the single chest hair, to the political correctness of 'Plagued One', this story manages to be hilarious and witty while remaining grounded in character. The protagonist's struggle with inadequacy and jealousy (even under such fraught circumstances) is instantly relatable and adds a layer of absurdity to the experience. And the final decision to kill 'someone else's darling' was the perfect response to this round's anti-prompt, and made Zombie Babe the standout for the April *Prize*.

Amanda's comments

One of the great joys of judging this competition is stumbling upon delightfully unhinged stories like this one.

Zombie Babe grabbed my attention from its incredibly hooking first paragraph and didn't let up until its dramatic conclusion. What might, on its surface, seem like a frivolous tale, proves by the end to be an incredibly well-executed piece of fiction.

What I think Louise did masterfully here is focus the reader's attention on highly interesting and relevant details: from the protagonist's 'one and only' chest hair to a preoccupation with Hollywood, every little thing is paid off to our immense satisfaction.

On top of that, we have a compelling narrative voice and vivid, sensory description, combined with artful circularity and a contagious sense of fun.

I'm sure Ed and I will be giggling about this story for a long time to come.

A BEACH, IF YOU COULD CALL IT THAT

Malte Springer

So a beach, if you could call it that. A narrow strip of shoreland wedged between basalt cliffs, maybe. Puffins, definitely, their black-and-white plumage poking out of rock crevices like mould on stale rye bread. Chanting, low and guttural, against the creamy orange of the setting sun.

So basalt cliffs, perhaps, and shoreland in between, and on it, humans, of course. An old-timer combing the coarse sand with her metal detector, hoping for a quarter amongst the electronic waste. And a father, and his teenage son, listening to the deep baritones of hundreds of puffins, their voices echoing from east to west, overlapping like the world's least talented a-cappella group.

So a racket of seabirds, and unlawfully disposed of electronic waste, probably, under the shoreline wedged between basalt cliffs, and on top of the eastern precipice, a couple acres of oceanfront property, sealed off, still in development. And a billboard, announcing to the puffins nesting underneath that this, too, will become human land, in time. And the father enjoying the birdsong like he always has, not noticing the tune has changed, but the son understands, immediately, instinctively.

So a narrow strip of shoreland, somewhere, and an oceanfront property encroaching on the puffins' habitat, and birds that once ruled over the vast coastland confined to the western bluff, perched together in their own droppings, drinking the same contaminated water. After a strained, final chorus, an infected puffin with thinning plumage stops mid-flight, as if burdened by an invisible weight, and so it begins.

So a teenager that has heeded the warning spilling down the basalt cliffs and fled, and puffins, flying erratically at first, then falling out of the sky like feathered cannon balls, and one of them strikes the old-timer, showering her metal detector in crimson droplets, and the father runs over to help, and so it spreads.

So a hundred strips of shoreland, and a hundred cliffs with oceanfront properties in various stages of development, and thousands of puffins dropping down like kamikaze pilots, and a hundred roads moving inland, sticky tar veins binding human life together like bubblegum hastily pressed between popsicle sticks, veins now transmitting deadly pathogens directly to its heart.

So a father that started coughing and faded away, and a son that becomes a father himself, later, for despite the birds' wrath he hasn't given up. But his resistance is in vain, because the puffins have been here since the Eocene, and humans have forgotten that, probably, and now it's their turn to be forgotten.

So an unread billboard on a basalt cliff touting progress that won't arrive, towering over a beach, if you could call it that, and an abandoned metal detector partly buried under the coarse sand, and silence, mostly.

And then, on the eastern precipice above a narrow strip of shoreland, a nest, maybe, and soft purring emanating from within, and after a while, the plumage of puffins emerging from basalt rock like the first petals of spring after winter.

About the author

Malte Springer, 34, is a PR editor and father of two from Leipzig, Germany. A couple years ago, he discovered flash fiction competitions as the ideal hobby, providing bursts of creative energy while also serving as a family-friendly outlet for his misplaced perfectionism and gambling proclivities. He's now a regular on the circuit, adding as many competitions (read: dopamine hits) as he can squeeze in between pesky distractions like play dates, vacations, or family gatherings.

Author's insights

'I've always seen myself more of an "ideas guy with editing skills" than a "writer." In micro fiction, this means I usually prefer high-concept or plot-heavy stories to more literary endeavors. Not surprisingly, I immediately homed in on a literal approach to the anti-prompt.

'The darlings killed in my editing are usually descriptions, and scenes that do not advance the plot. The idea of using repetition as the primary technique, slowly unfolding a scene by adding and re-mixing little pieces of description, was a fun concept to explore. The resulting journey from a beach to the end of humanity (and back to the beach) is meant to be read somewhere between a cautionary tale ("Could this happen one day?") and a fable ("Did this happen already?").

'I must thank my old friend Lukas who, years ago, shared with me his delightfully weird short story about frogs that, upon realizing the harmful effects of man-made global warming, rise from the swamps and go on a brutal killing spree. My kamikaze puffins are a direct result of that story being in my head for all these years.'

Ed's comments

What immediately captivated us about this piece was its poetic cadence and unusual narrative style. The repeated fragments hint at a larger story that feels uncertain, speculative, like a verbal history recounted years after a devastating pandemic. We may not have all the facts to understand the full story, but then, neither does the narrator. It's this uncertainty that creates intrigue, affecting an uneasy mood that stays with you.

Amanda's comments

Malte's bold, narrative voice in this piece was an instant standout, maintaining a firm grip on my imagination from the story's title to its final line.

This is a story that quite literally kills off all of humankind while preserving the 'darlings' of its prose—a perfect response to this round's anti-prompt.

As Ed noted, in his comments, it reads like a verbal history, rife with half-remembered details, and meandering in a way which feels intrinsically human, even as it imagines us long gone.

When the COVID-19 pandemic hit, it forced us to confront the stark plausibility of humanity's imminent demise. Just as teenagers think themselves invincible, perhaps the human race has long existed in a similar bubble?

So it's only now, through that collective wake-up call, we've matured enough to confront the consequences of our actions.

Maybe.

WANTED DEAD OR ALIVE: 'ARSON' ANDY & 'SHADOW' SHARON

Chloe Paige

Folks 'round here like to argue 'bout who's more deadly, Arson Andy or Shadow Sharon, but let me tell you there ain't nothing more deadly than a woman after her share of the money goes

up

in

flames.

And the folks are talking 'bout her when Sharon prowls into the saloon,

her hat pulled low,

keeping a wily, hand-to-cleaver mosey. They're cursing Shadow Sharon and her faceless wanted poster hanging on that wall over there. These folks only know

empty purses,

missing persons,

and never a ruckus, 'cause folks don't notice they have a shadow 'till it's too late.

But Sharon ain't near those folks no more, 'cause there's a man at the bar,

his hat pulled low,

keeping a shifty, hands-in-pocket silence. And Sharon's looking like a butcheress by day ready to take out that man over there. This woman only knows

robbing homes,

burying bones,

and never a hatchet, 'cause spilling blood was always a sealed kind of fate.

And the folks are talking 'bout her when Sharon follows that man to the general store,

her hat pulled low,

keeping a sneaky, hands-to-self distance. They're cursing Shadow Sharon and Arson Andy for having burned down that bank over there. These folks only know

empty cells,

burning smells,

and never no gossip, 'cause there ain't no way that fire-whirl bastard coulda snuck in without her aid.

But Sharon ain't near those folks no more, 'cause she follows that man to the abandoned jail,

her hat pulled low,

keeping a steady, hands-on-jerrycan malice. And Sharon's looking like she's 'bout to give that man a taste of his own petrol over there. This woman only knows

broken pacts,

stabbing backs,

and never her revenge, 'cause the butchered man she's dousing has a stranger's face.

And folks might still be talking 'bout her while Sharon gapes at the drunken decoy,

her hat pulled low,

keeping an antsy, hands-too-wet fumble. She's cursing Arson Andy for laying low after burning that bank before she could sneak her money outta there. This woman only knows

bills in ashes,

petrol splashes,

and never a morrow, 'cause the cell door is slamming shut behind this dust-devil woman.

But Arson Andy ain't near those folks no more, 'cause I'm here in the shadows,

my hat pulled low,

making a haughty, hand-on-flint entrance. And I'm looking like a gentleman by day who was never in it for the money. I only know

firebug thrills,

one-crook hills,

and always my manners, 'cause you never douse a darling, you let her do it herself.

Folks 'round here like to argue 'bout who's more deadly, Arson Andy or Shadow Sharon, but let me tell you there ain't nothing more dead than a woman with a shadow going

up

in

flames.

About the author

Living on Wadawurrung country in Geelong, Australia, Chloe daydreams professionally but aims to write a novel that exists beyond a first draft. Chloe has made appearances in *Flash Fiction Magazine*, *The Write-In*, and now this anthology right here in front of you! Don't make any sudden movements, she's easily spooked.

Chloe's work features twice in this anthology. You can find her other contribution on page 184.

Author's insights

'In a desperate bid to stand out, I set out to kill the judges' darlings. I took these two people from their families, gave them new identities, and dropped them off in the Wild West to fight it out. It was a real awkward car ride on the way there.

'All my writing darlings fell into the mix while I was drafting this story. There's too many to list, but I'm sure you'll find them. To keep my darlings alive without them weighing down the plot, I offset them with movement. The characters are always moving within the story. Meanwhile, the structure's rhyming couplets and fractured lines keep a steady rhythm.

'This was a challenge, but very fun to write. Not because I set someone on fire. I might need to say that for legal reasons.'

Ed's comments

Let me tell you, we were *dying* to discover the identity of this author, who left only a smiley face emoji as a calling card in her submission. Andy is Amanda's husband Sharon is my wife, so this response to the 'kill your darlings' anti-prompt felt deeply personal.

But once you have the judges' attention you still need to deliver on story, and *Wanted Dead or Alive* did so completely, with a strong voice that demands to be read in a stereotypical 'Wild West' accent (perhaps with a hint of Mt Druitt), beautiful phrasing, and a rich, character-driven plot.

We are thankful our real darlings remain safe.

Amanda's comments

What felt incredibly cool to me about this story was how Chloe instantly evoked that Wild West accent through her careful choice of words and ambling rhythm. You don't read this story; you mosey through it, legs akimbo and saddle-sore.

Beyond its narrative voice however, the story also delivers gripping plot, complete with a satisfying twist. It is an incredibly rare talent to be able to pack so much narrative into fresh-feeling rhyming couplets.

It's also a clever technique in the flash format: to maximise word count efficiency by taking what is familiar and instantly recognisable (a Wild West standoff), and imbue it with enough originality to make it stand out from the crowd. Colour me impressed.

Aside from all that, I feel it's incumbent on me to refute the claim that Andy is anything but a gentleman by day *and* night.

To my knowledge, he hasn't committed arson in *years*.

A PRIEST TO NO GOD

Taurenelle

Thirteen steps to the kitchen: five forward, three backward, six forward, two backward, one forward. But that was only when he thought about Sarah dying, which was nearly every morning. Otherwise, Dean's coffee was just seven steps away.

The teaspoon only ricocheted off the inside of the mug *once*, producing a single concussive sound, which was never enough to stop his son's school bus from skidding on black ice and flipping on its back as it collided with a speeding Mack Truck.

Three clinks. He needed to hear three clinks. But they couldn't be forced, either. A single tap should allow the sugar to fall from the spoon, and the displaced weight should propel his wrist like a pendulum, ringing in the subsequent twin chimes.

He had four teaspoons of sugar this morning. He preferred his coffee with *one*, but the bus needed to arrive safely before he could put on his jacket.

'Good luck with the pitch.' Sarah kissed his cheek before grabbing her purse and swallowing a handful of vitamins as she ran out the door.

How does she do that without water?

She was choking. In his mind…she was choking. And those vitamins weren't FDA-approved. They could cause cancer for all he knew. Sarah was choking to death during chemo. A scene that played out in his theater-of-one thousands of times before. He was eternally bound by the shackles of relentless thoughts, watching rehearsals for a show he never wanted to see. Praying for release.

But he couldn't ask her to change her routine. He always concealed his obsessions, though his compulsions were hard to ignore—making him late to work and awkward at parties. But Sarah loved him anyway.

And he couldn't imagine his life without her.

So, he slid his fingertips along the groove of the backsplash while quietly counting to seventeen. It used to be seven, but she had a particularly bad headache one day last year, and he'd lost ten more seconds of his life every morning since.

'Stop one ritual for one day,' the experts say. 'See what happens. See that everything will be okay.'

But what if it wasn't? What if one more *clink* could save his son from an unending coma? What if one more step keeps his wife from being stabbed at the supermarket? What if three perfectly aligned pencils could prevent a catastrophic stroke? How could he live with himself? He was sealing his family's fate with thirty-two flicks of a light switch. A small price to pay for peace of mind. How could he risk changing anything? Things needed to stay the way they were. Always. These ceremonies, these observances, mattered. They were—

—where was his wallet?

Right. In the dining room. Where his world was ending.

Five steps forward, three backward, six forward, two backward, one forward.

He sacrificed his time to a second cup of undrinkable coffee.

A priest to no god. A suppliant to a strange faith.

He was late for work again.

About the author

Taurenelle is a Pushcart Prize-nominated author and prosimetrist based in New York City. Excerpts from his fantasy manuscript, *Deep Lore*, earned him a spot on the 2024 Granum Foundation Longlist, and his heartbreaking tale, *I told you this was a poem*, won First Place in the October 2024 *Not Quite Write Prize for Flash Fiction*.

With a unique mixture of poetic prose, absurd humor, and deep world-building, his work aims to attract the casual reader and the analytical fantaphile alike (yes, he made that word up). A trained classicist, Taurenelle's narrative voice embodies the Roman and Ancient Greek poets of old, with a style that is simultaneously archaic and contemporary.

When he's not writing, he can be found sitting on his front stoop, wearing a full suit, reading Vergil, and drinking whiskey. Unless it's cold outside, then he can be found sitting in a library, wearing a full suit, reading Vergil, and hiding his whiskey from the librarians.

Author's insights

'The anti-prompt, "kill your darlings," stood out to me because it's advice that can be applied to more than just the writing process. While the obvious subversion of this prompt would be to either fill the piece with unnecessary details or have the characters literally kill something, I challenged myself to take a more meta approach.

'I wrote about OCD, a condition I have, because as someone who suffers from it, I can tell you that "killing your darlings" feels like an impossible task. The character in the story has two darlings, his loved ones, whom he obsessively worries about, and the compulsions he does because he fears he will bring harm to his family if he doesn't do them. Essentially, he fears that if he kills his darlings (the compulsions), it may result in indirectly killing his darlings (his loved ones).

'I named the piece "A priest to no god," not to be atheistic, which I am not, but to draw parallels to the orthopraxy of ancient Roman religion, in which if a ritual wasn't done flawlessly (say a word was missed or an animal made an inauspicious sound during the ceremony), they would start over from the beginning. Not that I would expect the reader to know any of this, it's just what inspired me because, personally, having OCD feels like that, it feels like being a priest to no god.'

Ed's comments

Taurenelle returns to the shortlist with a very introspective character study. We often advise avoiding internality in flash fiction as it can limit the dynamism necessary for powerful storytelling, but Taurenelle circumvents this issue by grounding his character's thoughts directly in the action of the scene (even if that action is as simple as stirring a cup of coffee). The subject of the main character Dean's OCD is treated directly, with compassion and without melodrama, allowing the reader to empathetically connect with his condition and the mental prison it creates.

Amanda's comments

I connected immediately with this story on a deep emotional level. Not because I have OCD (I don't) but because I love someone who battles the very same obsessive thinking and compulsive behaviour as the protagonist in this story.

The interiority of this story works here, because when it comes to OCD, every battle is fought entirely within one's own mind. By giving us a rare insight into this character's train of thought, Taurenelle invites our deep insight and empathy.

Although Taurenelle's protagonist wasn't quite able to kill his OCD darlings on this occasion (and in spite of my own apathetic agnosticism) I remain faithful that he *will* beat them in the end.

MY PERIPATETIC SOUL LONGS TO PLANT ITSELF BESIDE YOU

Jo Binns

Confession: since the moment we met, I've been trying to kill my darlings, my darling.

At first they were small, and though I longed to speak them, holding back was like swallowing watermelon seeds in the summertime. *Honey. Babe. Cutie-pie.* Just a syllable or two. No doubt they would disintegrate in my stomach acid.

On our fourth date, you snorted beer out your nostrils laughing at one of my cheesy jokes. My darlings turned ridiculous to fit the mood. *Pookie-pants. My charming little chookling-boots.* They rose alarmingly in my mouth, ready to reveal themselves, but just in time you left to the bathroom to wipe beer off your shirt. So I swallowed those darlings too, though they felt like peach pits rasping down my throat.

I dropped around to see you one afternoon in autumn, two months after we started dating. You were singing to your pot plants as you watered them. Sunlight filtered through the windows and your smile shone as you turned to ask me, 'What's your favourite watering song?'

We danced around your apartment singing 'Africa' by Toto at the top of our lungs and then I went to make us coffee so I could stand in your kitchen a moment and whisper whimsical darlings like *my mellifluous melody-maker* and *my perspicacious periwinkle*. I couldn't swallow them, they were too big. I pruned them ruthlessly, hoping they'd wither like a hacked-up rosebush.

You see, someone else killed my darlings, long ago. Cut them down when I said *dear*. Broke my heart when I said *I love you*. So I thought, with you, I'd kill them before you could.

I invited you around for dinner last night. Cooked all afternoon, set up candles, laid out shining silverware. You were late, arriving breathless with apology. 'I got stuck reading. Do you mind if I just sit a minute to finish this?' You held up *One Hundred Years of Solitude*. I'd told you it was my favourite book.

You looked so handsome and happy to see me, but by then I'd lost my nerve, so I sprayed this darling with pesticide: *you're the wave my heart surfs to shore upon.*

A heart sealed tight can never hurt. Or so I'd told myself. As you shut your finished book and grinned at me, I no longer thought that was true.

So before I left for work this morning, while you lay sleeping in my bed, I wiped my old shopping list off the little whiteboard in my kitchen and, hand shaking, wrote you a note. *Have a wonderful day, my darling.*

I'd done it.

Throughout the day, all those macheted, half-suffocated darlings breathed loudly in my ear. My own breath was short with anticipation. I was excited rather than scared. I knew I'd get a message back.

When I got home, my whiteboard read: *Good evening, my tenderhearted twinklebutt. Call me.* I danced around my kitchen as my not-killed darlings blossomed in a riotous bloom.

And then I called you.

About the author

Jo Binns lives in Melbourne, Australia. She likes staying fit, but is thwarted by a love of gin martinis, cheese, and sitting down to read. Jo's words can be found in *Crepuscular Magazine* and *Elegant Literature*, and a Bronze-awarded story in *ScribesMICRO*.

Author's insights

'One of my lovely friends gets easily embarrassed by any 'darling' talk, so her lovely husband makes up fun and ridiculous darlings to call her to keep her from getting shy. I always do a deep-dive exploration of each of the prompts, so when I started writing down some alternative ways of saying 'darling' it reminded me of my two friends. This made me happy, so I leaned in! The adoring statements between them are much more fun than what I came up with, though I am quite proud of "my tenderhearted twinklebutt"!

'This story started falling out of me as soon as I thought about someone trying to suppress their expressions of adoration and what might make someone want to do that, despite the fact that they have clearly met someone who is into them, and they are returning the feeling. I have to say I did tap into a few personal emotions for this one, though the story isn't at all non-fiction.

'I was really happy that I didn't have to kill any of my darlings—every little phrase I brainstormed made it in. I was worried about "my peripatetic soul longs to plant itself beside you," which was left over by the end, but then it became the title.

I had such a good time with this anti-prompt. Thank you, *Not Quite Write!*'

Ed's comments

Jo's unique response to the anti-prompt (one's 'darling' being the word 'darling') is a cute premise that really sells this charming and endearing little love story.

The idea of wrestling with emotional vulnerability after heartbreak is completely relatable. But elevating this story are the perfectly crafted and very specific anecdotes that develop character while simultaneously convincing us that our protagonist has made the right choice in allowing herself to become vulnerable once more.

Amanda's comments

Writing fiction, at least writing *good* fiction, is an act of immense vulnerability, which makes this story instantly relatable to any writer. We can all probably recall a time when our openness, our willingness to lay ourselves bare on the page, was clipped by a critic (well-meaning though they may have been... or not).

This story is as much a sweet romance as it is the redemption arc of every writer who has weathered rejection and found the courage to bare themselves once more.

I'm so glad I got to meet Jo's 'darlings' this round, and I can only encourage any other writer reading this to let your own darlings fly free from time to time. Who knows? They might find true love!

IN THE PALE MOONLIGHT

Greg Schmidt

The kangaroo is a silhouette against the moonlit paddock. Dad and I are in the tray of the ute. We do not speak, but our breath clouds in the night air. He nods, and I ready the rifle in my arms. Dad has bagged a few roos already tonight, but he's finally letting me take the shot. My finger hovers anxiously over the trigger.

Dad flicks a switch, and a beam of light bursts through the night, illuminating the kangaroo. Frozen in the spotlight, it appears unreal, like a statue. I am reminded of the stuffed kangaroo I used to sleep with. On hot nights its plastic eyes were cool against my skin. I shake off the memory. That toy is sealed away in some box now, forgotten with other childish things. Dad says roos are pests, and there's no place for them on the farm. I pull the trigger, and the kangaroo falls from the spotlight.

'Got it!' I cry. 'Did'ya see, Dad?'

'I saw. Let's go check.'

Dad drives through the paddock. Behind us rattles a trailer with the carcasses of tonight's earlier kills. Ahead, bright headlights stretch like fingers through the shadows, and a grim uneasiness grows within me. Out of the darkness, the fallen kangaroo appears, stark in the white light. It lays on its side, and steam rises from a bullet hole in its head. Dad leaves the headlights on, and we get out.

'Nice shot, son.'

I'd expected pride at Dad's praise, but it's lost before the ugly reality of my own action. Not wanting Dad to see me flinch, I approach the kangaroo to make sure it's dead. The beast's belly ripples with motion, and I recoil.

'It's alive!'

A tiny nose pokes out of the kangaroo's pouch. Two black eyes follow, shining in the headlights, and wide with fright.

'No,' says Dad. 'It was a Mum.'

'What do we do?'

'It gets the same, son, less the bullet.'

Dad stands over the dead kangaroo. The joey tries to squirm back into the pouch, but Dad reaches in and pulls it out forcefully. He grips its back legs, and the joey wriggles as it hangs suspended upside down.

'B…but, Dad. It's only a kid.'

'So? It's a pest just the same, and you weren't so shy to put a bullet in its Mum.'

I drop my head, and Dad raises the joey in the air. He swings it down hard, smashing its head against the ute's bull bar. A loud clang echoes across the paddock. The joey hangs limp in Dad's hand.

'You want the farm someday? Here's the reality.' Dad offers me the joey. 'Put it with the rest.'

I take it in my arms, surprised by the weight, and carry it to the trailer. I place the joey on the other dead kangaroos, and it nestles amongst them. It could almost be sleeping if not for its black eyes, open and unmoving. In the pale moonlight, they look like plastic.

About the author

Greg Schmidt is a writer from Western Sydney. His story, *Untitled #2*, shortlisted in the inaugural *Not Quite Write Prize for Flash Fiction*, and was featured in last year's anthology.

Primarily writing short and flash fiction, Greg enjoys experimenting with various genres and themes. Recently, he has found voice with stories about how animals make us feel and about how we treat them in turn. And there's still some about farts, too.

Greg's work features twice in this anthology. You can find his other contribution on page 46.

Author's insights

'I wasn't sure how to handle this anti-prompt in a traditional sense, so I thought about areas outside of writing where we "kill our darlings". I was inspired by a mob of kangaroos near where I live who are being displaced due to expanding housing estates, and it led me to consider how we view and treat the kangaroo in Australia.

'As one of our most iconic native animals, our darling if you will, we often don't afford them that reverence, instead viewing them as pests on farms, or as unwanted obstacles for new developments. Frequently, the solution is to just have them killed.

'I wanted to contrast this viewpoint against a more compassionate one, and a father/son dynamic seemed the perfect parallel in a small word count. I felt this relationship, particularly of a child struggling with the expectations of the parent, would be very recognisable and serve to enhance the impact.'

Ed's comments

Greg has pivoted from fart-cutes and magical faecal Scotsmen to something far more serious and grounded.

We loved the visceral reality of these scenes, conjuring vivid images of nocturnal Kangaroo hunting, à la *Wake in Fright*. But it's the emotional resonance that really makes this piece hit hard, like the comparison between a child's stuffed toy and the eyes of a dead animal, signifying the death of childhood innocence and an acceptance of the amoral realities of life. It's a trade-off that we are never truly comfortable with.

Amanda's comments

Some of my fondest childhood memories involve visiting the farm where my father grew up and going feral with my cousins for a few days.

It's life and death on a farm. I can still see my younger cousins stumbling on an abandoned bird's nest and doing their best to rescue the frail hatchlings. Just as vividly, I recall the cockatoo (a reviled pest to the resident farmer), head shot clean off by a single rifle bullet, lifeless claws holding fast to a high branch of the tallest pine.

The cognitive dissonance we rely on to distance ourselves from 'how the sausage is made' shields us from the stark realities Greg invites us to confront in this story. Farming is its own kind of war, and the pests are the enemy.

I returned, alone, to my Dad's old family farm just last year. It's abandoned now—sold to a mining company to make way for a mere six kilometre bypass to the quarries. The convict-hewn stone of the house, the memories and ghosts trapped in its walls, never stood a chance of heritage-listing in the face of 'progress'.

It's true: the only constant in life is change. And in this story, Greg captures, perfectly, the sting in its tail.

APRIL 2025 LONGLIST

The following list represents the remaining longlisted entries, in no particular order:

- **WILDCARD WINNER** – A NEW BLOOM by Lisa Vitale
- **WILDCARD WINNER** – PARROT IN A BLENDER by J. R. Lowe
- **WILDCARD WINNER** – CHOICES by Thom Brodkin
- RESETS AND REDEMPTIONS by Jaden Christopher
- TAR by Ben Daggers
- INFESTATION by Steven Huff
- A BOX BENEATH THE ROSEBUSH by Theo Carr
- BALLOON GUY by KR Emmanuel
- THE SANDCASTLE TEST by Phoebe Robertson
- THE NECROMANTIC OATH by Georgina Maxine
- LAUGHTER IS THE SIXTH STAGE OF GRIEF by Natalie Bucsko
- GRIMOIRE SHE WROTE by SJ Snyder

- THE PETER PAN WEDDING MASSACRE by GeorgeD
- SKELETONS IN THE CLOSET by Lucy Mac
- THE ART by Harry Humber
- THE REOCCURRING RESURRECTION OF ALASTAIR EMRYS, PART THIRTEEN by Kris Schnebelen
- ONE SMALL STEP by Ella Micallef
- WIP_FINAL.DOC by Corrie Haldane
- THE AMBIGUITY OF IDENTITY: JUST WHO ARE YOU, CARLA? by W. J. Arthur
- BORROWED TIME by Eloise Keary
- CRIME SEEN by Berni Rushton
- CREEPY CLOWN FOR THE WIN by A. J. Blackman
- CHALK SISTER by Holly Brandon
- NIGHT DRIVER by Sarah Jordan
- AFTER THE UNDOING by Athena Law
- THE MOON IS A PLACE YOU CAN GO by Kelli Johnson
- ALL I'VE GOT ARE MENTHOLS by Farrah Pascal
- THE OTHER ONE PERCENT by Emma Makarova
- ALL THE TIMES I SAW CARL NAKED by Christy Hartman
- TO FILL A FOX by Chloee Thornhill
- PICKLING MEMORIES by MM Schreier
- THE SILENCE, THE SEA, AND THE BURNING STARS by Alexandria Bellani
- PETTY KALE by Autumn Bettinger

- HOARDERS SEASON 36, EPISODE 7 by Ashleigh Adams

Note: Each judge has awarded a wildcard prize to an entry which did not make the shortlist but which we otherwise felt deserved recognition. This round, our new assistant judge, Dean Koorey, was invited to award a third wildcard prize.

JULY

2025

Overview

The July 2025 *Not Quite Write Prize for Flash Fiction* challenged writers to create an original piece of fiction of no more than 500 words, which:

included the word **CRANE**.

included the action **'burning something'**.

broke the writing rule, **'Use active voice.'**

The competition drew **340 entries** from authors in a reported **16 countries** around the world. That's **163,821** words for our judges to read. That's about the same number of words as ***Frankenstein* by Mary Shelley**.

Please enjoy the following top six stories from this round of the competition…

FOLD. BURN. INHALE.

Elda Orozco

The paper crane had been folded on the night of her funeral. His hands, rigid with grief, had pressed each crease hard and fast, as if he could force life into it. When he set it on the windowsill, the moonlight caught its frame, and its wings fluttered as if alive, releasing a hint of ink and her perfume.

'Richard, you shouldn't have done that,' her voice whispered from the paper. He laughed through tears, pressing the crane to his lips like a sacrament.

'If I fold a thousand birds, will you stay with me?'

'Maybe.'

For weeks, Nina stayed with him. A ghost in origami, perched on his pillow. At night, she nestled against his neck, her sharp beak pricking his pulse point like a reminder of life. The voice was hers, but her body was *wrong*. Where her pink softness had once contoured against him, now she was no more than grey geometry.

'You could unfold me,' she teased as she traced his collarbone with the razor-edge of one wing.

He tried, once. His quivering fingers pried at her seams, but she spread into sharp, parched planes. She wasn't flesh, but a delicate thing, a prison of lines where curves should be.

'I want more,' he muttered, though the way she tilted her head, exactly like her, made his chest ache. 'I want to feel you.' He sobbed as he refolded her.

But grief didn't take away the hunger.

At dawn, he slid the crane between his lips, letting her voice vibrate against his. He wanted to soften her. To make her moan like she had under his hands. To feel her skin, but his lips came away damp. Not with glue, but with salt, as if she'd been crying.

Time passed, but he couldn't move on. Nina had grown weak in his palms, like a love letter left in the rain.

He tried everything—kisses, blood, breath—but paper couldn't love him back. *Not yet.*

One night, delirious and desperate, Richard held her over a candle.

'Yes,' she hissed as the flickering flame licked her.

The sheet curled like a living soul, her edges blackened, as if the heat had loosened her. And for a fractured second, she was pliant in his hands, until the fire swallowed her whole. Ash curled upward, not in smoke, but in sinuous shapes spiraling around him. Without hesitation, he inhaled, and his lungs were filled with her. Her laughter tickled within, and a smile appeared on his lips as she kissed his bloodstream.

He stood before the mirror, watching Nina's silhouette move beneath his skin like a second shadow.

'Nina, I can feel you. Can you feel me?'

Her answer was the press of phantom lips to his pulse, the glide of her hands (his hands?) down his stomach.

Outside, snow fell. Inside, they burned.

And for once, the hunger was satisfied.

About the author

Elda Orozco conjures stories where myth bleeds into the modern and words become a haunting. Her work, nestled between magical realism and the uncanny, explores primal hungers and contradictions that define our humanity.

Author's insights

'A paper crane was an obvious choice to pair with the action of "burning something". I decided to use passive voice in key moments to mimic grief's theft of agency, where characters are acted upon, echoing the story's heart: Love as both possession and surrender.

'Then I let myself wonder: if we are an immortal soul inhabiting a body, would it be enough to remain incorporeal and anchored to those we love? Or perhaps there is a primal hunger to feel their presence.

'I decided to explore the agony of missing not just a soul, but the female form—the memory of its weight, its softness, its contours. The origami crane, with its harsh, precise lines, became the perfect symbol of this deprivation: a sharp, painful reminder of the curves that are absent. The story is about the uncanny horror of a lover's voice emanating from a form that is all angles, and the desperate, alchemical need for a love so consuming that it must be inhaled.'

Ed's comments

The July round brought dozens of stories featuring origami cranes, but none with greater depth of emotional energy as Elda's winning entry. The peculiar ways Richard deals with his grief somehow amplify this energy, making everything feel more urgent, more real. The climax is that exquisite burning moment, in which he is able to finally connect with her once more.

An absolute slam-dunk that centres all three prompts.

Amanda's comments

This story feels incredibly intimate, like a whispered secret accompanied by a subtle hiss that warns of the danger of going in too deep.

It is an unhinged premise, to be sure—a lover trapped in the folds of a paper crane—but that strangeness is built upon a deep, recognisable truth: the irrational bargains we make in the face of grief.

Every moment of this story feels laced with risk, and what I enjoyed most was how Elda didn't pull any punches with that ending. She allows Richard to lose himself, and us as readers to fall off the cliff with him.

CHECKING YOU OUT: ROMANCE AT REGISTER 3

Ella Micallef

Packet of gum, Caesar salad mix, a single banana.

Each is placed with precision, tanned fingers drumming on the conveyor.

'MJ,' he reads, squinting at my name badge. 'Cool name, what's it short for? Mary Jane?'

'Um, no,' I clear my throat. I scan the gum. *Beep.* 'My parents just... liked the letters? Together?'

He flicks auburn hair from his eyes, and it falls back to where it was.

Beep – one banana. *Does this mean he's single?*

'At least it's a good conversation starter – mine's Adam.'

'Oh... what's that short for?'

He cocks his head and his smile tilts sideways, and I wish the building would collapse.

'Nothing, my parents just liked the letters together.'

Adam's grin does nothing to douse the embarrassment burning my cheeks.

***

Packet of flower seeds, chicken and lettuce sandwich, one banana.

I scan the seeds, mind scrambling for something clever to say. 'Cool, seeds! They for planting?'

Adam fights a smile. 'How *do* you always guess these things? I'm hoping to attract the birds.'

'And the banana? You planting that too?' The *beep* of the banana being scanned is excruciatingly loud. His nose screws up as he emits a perfect snort.

'Nope, just a snack.'

'Oh, right. Because it's food. For eating. Do you want a bag?'

'Nah, I'm alright, thanks.'

He turns, and I crane my neck to watch him go. I wish I could grab his face and kiss his gorgeous flower-planting—

'See you tomorrow, MJ.'

***

Spiral pasta, fresh basil, one banana.

Of all the registers, his food appears at mine.

'Hi! Adam! How are you?' My voice cracks like a teenage boy's. *Real smooth.*

He smiles distractedly, pulling out his leather wallet.

'What's the basil for? Is it—do you eat it... raw? Or are you making a... basil thing?'

He half-grins, eyes shifting to check his phone. 'Pesto. I'm making pesto pasta.'

Images flash before me; this perfect man cooking me pesto pasta, eyes locking over glasses of chardonnay...

Beep. Beep. Beep.

'Fancy.' I pass his banana.

'What, the banana?'

'No, the pasta,' I wring my hands beneath the counter. 'Banana's cool though – loads of potassium...'

Adam's lips twitch, eyes averted. My heart plummets.

'Too true, MJ, gotta keep the potassium levels up.'

*****

Eye fillet steaks, potato salad, two bananas.

Two bananas.

Beep. Beep. Silence.

My chest is full of stones and my mouth betrays me. 'Who's the lucky girl?' I blurt. 'Or guy, or... monkey...?'

He snorts, grabbing his groceries. 'You know me too well, MJ!' he calls over his shoulder.

On the bench, one banana, neglected in his thoughts of someone else.

'Wait, Adam! You forgot your—'

He swivels, eyes locked in the fluorescent glow of the sliding doors.

I raise the fruit, and that's when I catch sight of them: ten digits etched upon the skin.

Adam fumbles with his banana, holds it to his ear and mouths two words into the curve.

Call me?

About the author

Ella Micallef is a young writer who lives with her family on the Gold Coast. A lover of books, she has been writing stories since before she could hold a pencil. In her short career, Ella has been shortlisted in the 2023 *Brisbane Writers Festival Microfiction Competition*, and proudly holds the title of being Amanda's first Wildcard winner in 2024. She has entered every single *Not Quite Write Prize for Flash Fiction* round, and will not stop until she wins first place. Or goes broke trying.

Author's insights

'As the urban legend goes, if you prominently display a single banana in your trolley, it indicates that you are single – or so my dad told me when I started working as a checkout operator. *Checking You Out: Romance at Register 3* was my first try at romantic fiction, which was very different to some of the themes I've previously written. All characters and events are entirely fictional, but the awkwardness is unfortunately 100% me.

'I did not expect this story to get as far as it did, as I cringed while writing every scene. Though, when I verbalised my idea for the ending, my parents said, "No, that's so bad… you have to write it." And they were right – it was bad in the best way. The banana phone was drawn from real life: my mum used to etch numbers into a banana's skin with a toothpick, so when it came to lunch, I had a fully non-functioning banana phone.

Hearing my name read out for the second-place prize was an emotional moment I won't forget easily.

'Disclaimer: Despite working predominantly at register 3, I have never come across a cute guy with a single banana. I'll keep my eyes peeled.'

Ed's comments

We were completely charmed by this supermarket meet-cute. The repetition and awkward dialogue build tension and drama, and the build-up is paid off perfectly when 'Chekhov's banana' goes off in the final scene. Is there a person alive who could resist such a smooth move?

Amanda's comments

I was beyond thrilled when we revealed the names of our shortlisted authors this round, and Ella's was among them.

Ella was my first ever wildcard pick in January 2024. Although she is very young, she went on to crack the *Not Quite Write Prize for Flash Fiction* longlist in April, backing it up here with a decisive shortlisting. It's an impressively rapid rise to fame, and one we're proud to be a part of.

I'm a little embarrassed to confess that the final line of this story gave me goosebumps. Turns out, I'm a sucker for bouncy, believable dialogue, and a very real-feeling meet-cute! Having said that, it's possible I would not exist had it not been for my parents' own *Coles* checkout meet-cute, so perhaps it's in my DNA?

Beyond this personal connection, what really struck me here was the perfect rom-com plot structure, with every detail working towards that climactic moment.

We often advise authors to stick to a single, pivotal scene in their stories, but Ella's use of a single setting and repeated banana device work in harmony to cover a longer period within the same condensed word count. This is perfect for a love story in which the relationship requires a little more time to develop.

If this is Ella's starting point as an author, I see big things in her future. I, for one, will be watching this space.

BIN BOY

Sam James

In moments of low self-esteem, I tell myself to get in the bin.

It's all I deserve, really. I'm a dirty little bin boy, incapable of doing anything right. I'm selfish and lazy, and succumb too easily to the instinctive inaction brought on by anxiety.

Yesterday we argued; apparently, I never offer to make her breakfast.

'You never offer to make me breakfast,' she said.

I took the accusation dumbly. It's true. My morning coffee is a pseudo-sacred ritual, a personal communion. I cannot bear interruptions when measuring and grinding the beans, pouring a spiral from my special gooseneck kettle. It's a daily moment of solemn reflection. Now it seems just another way I let her down.

Bin boy.

Even in this framing, it's about me. The cruel irony of low self-esteem is the amount of time spent thinking about oneself. '*I* never make her breakfast'. Perhaps rather: '*She* never has breakfast made for her'. Less something to blame myself for, more a manageable problem to tackle.

Today, I burnt the toast. Reframe: the toast was burnt. By me.

Such a romantic wake-up call, a smoke alarm. She emerges to quite a sight: me, dishevelled and shamefaced, knife in hand and a blanket of blackened scrapings covering a surprisingly large area of the counter.

Without missing a beat, she climbs a chair, deactivates the alarm, and opens a window. Why didn't I think to do that?

'Thanks for breakfast,' she says, kissing my cheek. 'Salvage what you can, I'll get ready.'

I clean up, and notice the bin is overfull. There's a small win—I can solve that, if nothing else. I tie the bag and take it out to the driveway, mulling on my shortcomings as I go.

The rubbish goes in the bin.

I go in the bin.

I'm not really cognisant of it as it's happening, only snapping into awareness as the lid closes above me. I don't know why, but the reek of old coffee grounds, rotting veg and miscellaneous refuse is somehow comforting, like I'm meant to be here. The rank condensation on the walls of the bin seeps through my clothes.

I hear the lorry further up the street. Collection day. Wheelie bins are being craned, hoisted, swallowed whole. If I stay quiet, maybe they'll swallow me.

As I contemplate what it would like to be compacted, the lid creaks open.

'There you are,' she says. 'It's bin day.'

'Yep.'

She considers me, huddled and soaked in self-pity, and shuts the lid. The world tilts, and I am wheeled to the street, bumped down a kerb.

A hysterical laugh, raw and unexpected, tears through me— a sudden realisation of the utter absurdity of hiding in a wheelie bin.

Halfway up the road, a bin man pauses. 'What was that?'

She gives the lid a firm, possessive thump. 'It's my bin boy!' I can hear her smiling.

She's right, I'm a dirty little bin boy—selfish, lazy. Covered in bin juice. But that doesn't matter.

I'm hers.

About the author

Sam James is a professional musician and amateur everything else from England. His writing's been featured almost nowhere—you can officially say you knew him before he went mainstream. Say you liked his blue period best, that'll impress the dinner guests. He is a proud member of the writing group *Up Down Left Write*.

Author's insights

'Look, I'm not saying I am the eponymous Bin Boy, nor that the other character is my partner, Rosie. I have certainly never crawled into a wheelie bin. But the kindness-in-the-face-of-absurdity that Bin Boy receives at the end of this story is something that Rosie shows me on a daily basis.

'Sometimes your own head is a bin, and we all need someone to open the lid a bit. If this story is about anything, it's that small mercies matter: a lifted lid, a steady hand, a laugh at the right moment. They're what help you climb back out.'

Ed's comments

Relatability can be extremely compelling in flash, and there's something supremely relatable about this absurdist reflection on burnt toast. Truly, we have all wanted to get in the bin at one time or another in our lives, but Sam has dared to take us all the way. And the cherry on top: his wife seems to agree that he belongs there!

Amanda's comments

Despite being completely ridiculous, this is nonetheless a sublime little story about loving someone exactly as they are.

Sam often wanders into the absurd, and it's a clever tactic in a flash fiction competition. Fiction gives writers permission to push reality to its limits, and it gives readers the opportunity to safely explore what might happen if we finally let our intrusive thoughts win. What could be more thrilling?

The real magic, which Sam handles effortlessly, is grounding that absurdity in a universal truth, so the character's choices feel not only understandable but almost, *almost*, rational.

A MEASURED DISTANCE

Alisa Coddington

No one had told them to look, but they all craned anyway.

Not all at once. A glance, then again. Soon the neighborhood developed a subtle lean. Not physical—just something about how people paused before entering their cars. Before unlocking the front door. The way conversations left space for interruption.

Whatever it was, it had already ended. Probably.

And yet, something above the rooflines refused to clear. Not a figure. Not movement. Just a texture in the air. A slight wrongness. Like a breath taken at the wrong time.

Ash showed up in odd places. On windshields. Inside closed drawers. A fine grit on the inside rim of drinking glasses. No one saw flames, but the smell was consistent. Sharp, synthetic—like the inside of a burned wire.

A note appeared on a lamppost. Weathered, folded. Typewritten.

If you looked, you've been seen.

If you looked away, it knows the shape of your refusal.

Nothing above forgets.

They looked because it was there. Or it was there because they looked.

People read it. No one removed it. After a few days, it blurred—still legible, but somehow altered. Some said the text moved slightly when you weren't looking.

A girl stood still in her yard one morning, arms raised—not waving. Not reaching. Just raised.

Her mother called her name twice. Then she just asked, 'Why?'

The girl said, 'It's measuring the distance.'

Her mother didn't ask again. That night she couldn't sleep—kept checking the curtains, fingers tight on the fabric as if pulling harder would hold the house together.

One man climbed up to clean his gutters and came down pale. Said there were pine needles where there shouldn't be pines. That the sky felt 'more personal up there'.

He left the next day. Didn't pack. Just kept driving, like if he stopped, it might notice.

The Jensen house gained a shadow with inconsistent edges. It stretched toward windows that had long since been covered.

The bulletin board at the post office began curling at the edges. Flyers faded faster than normal. Thumbtacks rusted overnight. Someone suggested humidity. No one confirmed.

An instinct. Like crossing a room with the lights off and not wanting to confirm what's in the corner.

And yet, sometimes, a person still forgets. Pauses mid-step. Head tilts. Just for a second. A flicker of curiosity. Of recognition.

They still check the curtains, fingers tight on the fabric. But by now, everyone understands—it isn't what's outside that waits.

It's the distance itself that's being measured.

And the distance always moves closer.

About the author

Alisa Coddington writes fiction from Minneapolis. She started writing later in life and is drawn to the overlooked edges of the everyday, with an eye toward what shifts just before it's named. This is her first publication.

Author's insights

'This story began with the image of a neighborhood leaning, as if something unseen was pressing against it. I've always been drawn to those in-between spaces where the ordinary feels slightly off, where people sense a shift but avoid naming it.

'I only started writing recently, after years of just carrying these observations around. Entering this contest pushed me to put one of them on the page and share it. For me, the story lives in that pause between looking and not looking... an uncertainty that feels like both hesitation and recognition.'

Ed's comments

One of the unique powers of the written word as compared to more visual art forms is its ability to tap directly into imagination, conjure images that are indefinite, ambiguous and ethereal. What exactly does 'measuring the distance' mean? We can only guess, but the idea of something seen yet unseen, of a hidden space 'in-between' seems like something out of *Close Encounters of the Third Kind*, *A Quiet Place* or *Stranger Things*, and it fills us with the same spooky, mystical feeling.

This story is pure atmosphere.

Amanda's comments

In my opinion, the best stories make us *feel* something. And this one made me feel very nervous.

What I loved most about it was its cinematic quality. Ed and I often talk on the podcast about 'dropping us into the scene', and Alisa appears to have mastered the art. I was immersed from the first word to the last, equal parts awed and puzzled by this mysterious threat.

Of course, fear feeds on uncertainty, and it's the *not knowing* in this story that allows our overanxious imaginations to run wild.

I feel so honoured to have helped bring Alisa's work to the world for the first time in this anthology. I can't wait to see what other gems her creativity unearths!

THE ONE

Holly Brandon

You arrive at the party twenty minutes late in a seen-better-decades minivan. With chipped-polish nails, you scrape a price sticker from the box of Legos you purchased on the way here and shove it into a ripped bag that was gifted to your son last month.

You find a hairbrush on the floormat that hasn't seen a vacuum in weeks and rake it through your son's tangles, his protesting screams mingling with your own forced-calm retort—'Well if you'd brushed your hair at home like you were told, I wouldn't have to do it for you.'

You rub lotion on razor-burnt legs that were shaved in the sink this morning, dab drugstore concealer under eyes that are never closed for more than five hours at a time. You brush cracker crumbs from your son's shirt, kiss his sticky cheek, taking his little hand in yours as you lead him to the bounce house in the backyard.

And as I sit in a folding chair, silent next to chattering moms who all somehow know each other (how do they always already know each other?), I watch you and I think—*are you the one?*

The one whose interests surpass potty training and sight words—the one who will help me strip the burnt edges and charred layers baked on by parenthood. Another alien in this strange world that didn't wait for us to catch up, who understands that while we'll always be mothers, we've been people even longer.

Your son bumps into a table, knocking several cupcakes to the ground, and as you crane your neck to see if anyone noticed, you step on a cupcake and whisper, 'Shit.'

I grab a stack of napkins and think—*please be the one.*

About the author

Holly Brandon is the world's okay-est wife, a terrible housekeeper, and the stay-at-home mom of four adorably feral children. She was born and raised in the Deep South of the U.S. and enjoys silence, chocolate, and mind-numbing television.

She has what some might call an unhealthy addiction to writing competitions, placing first in *Writers' Playground*, third in the *Henshaw Press Short Story Competition*, and third in *Flash 500's Short Story Competition*.

Holly also has stories published with *Flash Frog, Fairfield Scribes, Elegant Literature, the National Flash Fiction Day Anthology,* and *The Edinburgh Anthology.*

Author's insights

'This story almost didn't happen. My five-year-old daughter was released from a 3-day hospital visit (she is totally fine now, thank goodness!) a few days before the contest kicked off, so I'd planned on sitting out this round. However, I have an annual pass, and I hate not using things I've already paid for, so I stubbornly decided to pull something together at the last minute.

'The anti-prompt inspired me to include some version of the phrase, "If you'd done as you were told..." which is a quintessential parenting mantra. And in order to get something submitted quickly, I went with something that felt so natural and personal that it was practically autobiographical.

'I feel like I was describing myself in both characters of my story— I am 100% that frazzled minivan mom who's always late, and I am also the awkward mom who feels like I don't quite fit in with the other moms. But what I've found is that when you open up to other parents, you learn that most of them feel the exact same way. And sharing those insecurities and less-than-perfect admissions of guilt is a great way to find likeminded friends. We are all just trying to survive out here!'

Ed's comments

Parents will, of course, immediately recognise this specific scenario. But I'm sure we've all had the experience, in this performative world of ours, of being in a social situation and absolutely *craving* real, human connection. Holly captures the essence of this deep desire more directly and succinctly than I've seen before, while at the same time making the parents among us feel very seen.

Amanda's comments

We never grow out of it, do we? That social anxiety—the desire to fit in. This story *so* beautifully captures the intensity of this desire (a desire I share) that it gave me goosebumps.

Interestingly, it's through this character's perception of the others around her that we begin to form a picture of her. It's a picture to which many parents can relate. Naturally, we all see ourselves as the awkward outsider, perhaps never knowing how we are perceived by those around us.

Building on this relatable premise, Holly has delivered an emotional punch in fewer than 300 words. What parent doesn't long for help to 'strip the burnt edges and charred layers baked on by parenthood'?

Holly's short-but-sweet story provides yet another prime example of how powerful fiction can be when we derive our stories from a place of authenticity.

ANOTHER CHILD HAS BEEN KILLED IN PALESTINE

Justin Creps

Why the fuck am I still awake?

I work in five hours. My wife is sleeping peacefully beside me, and our son, Simon, is tucked in his crib, breathing barely audible breaths that crackle through the monitor's static. Our house is quiet, the room dark, except for my face, which glows white. I tap my phone's screen.

The following post contains graphic imagery that may be upsetting to some users.

I already know what it is. Amir, my friend from college, only posts about one thing.

Another child has been killed in Palestine.

I have a few friends who post about it regularly. One horrendous tragedy after another, innocent lives destroyed. They're always at the top of my feed, waiting for me when I open the app. My phone's facial recognition must notice my eyes lingering; the algorithm always knows.

Amir is braver than me, as I hide in the shadows of my bedroom, heart aching, voice silent, fingers still. Sentiment is worth nothing when you're too scared to speak. Too passive to act.

What am I afraid of?

Could I lose my job? A friendship? My reputation? Could I end up blacklisted by our increasingly fascist government? Is someone monitoring my online activity? Has an AI program analyzed every word I've ever posted?

Probably not. I'm just a fucking coward.

The girl's pink Velcro shoes hang limp from her father's arms as he runs through a city street, screaming guttural screams. She was Simon's age. Her brown eyes stare lifeless; black hair, matted with blood, clings to her face. The man is hysterical, pleading in a language I can't comprehend, yet as a father, I somehow understand. He's living my worst nightmare. An image of Simon, body torn to pieces, forms in my mind. I look away.

Then, I tap the screen.

Next post: before-and-after satellite images of Gaza. Pristine beaches, schools, and parks reduced to rubble, debris, and ash—burning in real-time. I look out my window at unending suburban sprawl. They're building *another* apartment complex—crane at the ready. Always expanding—always growing—more and more and more. One part of the world prospers while another is erased. I taste vomit.

I want to look away; ignore it; give into the excuses; stay silent. What could I possibly do anyway? Call a representative who doesn't care? Vote in a gerrymandered election? March in another pointless protest? None of it would matter. That's the awful truth. We can't do anything... and I can keep hiding behind that.

But there's no denying another truth I know without seeing. While I've been laying here, staring at my screen...

Another child has been *fucking killed* in Palestine.

I want to think tomorrow will be different. Maybe I'll find the courage to speak, like Amir, sharing uncomfortable truths.

But probably not.

This isn't a fairy tale. There's no redemption arc for me. This is real life, and I'm just a coward, scrolling on my phone.

At least now I know why the fuck I am awake.

About the author

Justin Creps is an engineering instructor and running coach from Central Ohio who writes character-driven speculative fiction that focuses on the emotional impact of identity and connection. Common elements in his stories include parent-child relationships, the afterlife, and consequences of technology.

When he's not teaching, coaching, or writing, he's often training for marathons, recording/editing his writing podcast (*Writing in Progress*), or being the best husband/father he can for his wife and two sons.

You can find a record of Justin's previously published work and accomplishments on his author website justincreps.com.

Author's insights

'As I brainstormed for creative ways to break the rule, "Use active voice," the fragment "has been killed" popped into my head early on. It felt like an emotionally resonant place to go while weaving the prompt fully into the plot. At some point, "a child has been killed" appeared on my idea list, and that's when the direction of my story became obvious to me, given the many instances of child death I've seen on social media over the last year.

'The last time I entered the *Not Quite Write Prize for Flash Fiction*, the anti-prompt to break was, "Write what you know," and I listened and learned from the shortlist, longlist, and daredevil episodes as Ed and Amanda analyzed how many stories from that competition did not feel authentic. *Another Child has been Killed in Palestine* is the most authentic and raw story I've ever submitted to anything, as it's really a reflection of my own fear for the consequences of speaking out, and the guilt that goes along with the resulting passivity. Full disclosure: I was pretty afraid to even attempt writing this story.

'So, the second (and, in my opinion, more meaningful) way I addressed "passive voice" was by making a character's struggle with their own reluctance to speak the main conflict. In a way, the fact that this story has been published and read aloud on a podcast is my own way of breaking through that struggle, which is pretty cool. I absolutely need to mention and thank my braver friends than I, who served as inspiration to write this story. "Amir" represents about a half-dozen people in my life who aren't afraid to speak out. In my opinion, "killing innocent children is wrong," shouldn't be a controversial take.

'I hope this story has broader appeal, as well. I aimed to capture the helplessness we feel in the face of terrible things beyond our control. I think a lot of readers can relate to that feeling, regardless of the specific horrible occurrence those frustrations may be directed towards. Sadly, it seems there are a lot to choose from these days, which undoubtedly affected my headspace as I was brainstorming for this competition. I leaned into it.'

Ed's comments

Justin's story captures something that many of us are feeling in the age of social media: we're confronted by disturbing images every day and expected to go about our lives as if everything is normal. Judged by some for not caring enough, and by others for caring too much, we are left to feel shame and wonder what it is we can actually do about a conflict on the other side of the world. We hold images of their suffering in our hands. We feel it's important to be informed, to see and acknowledge what is happening to real people, just like us. But do we have the tools to help them, or ourselves?

Amanda's comments

There were a number of excellent stories vying for the coveted final spot on the shortlist this round, however what came through very strongly in this piece, and what ultimately earned this story its place, was its deep emotional truth. I happen to share Justin's sentiment that, 'killing innocent children is wrong,' should never be a controversial take.

We often advise authors to avoid excessive interiority and focus instead on the action of the scene, however this highly interior piece succeeded specifically because of the deep insight it provides into the character's internal conflict. As readers, we are provided a clear dramatic question at the outset of the story ('Why the fuck am I still awake?'), with our reading satisfaction assured as we work through that inner conflict to arrive at a clear answer (albeit a sad one) by the end.

Not all stories have happy endings, and humanity will always possess an entropic quality that assures its own demise. Still, while we're all on this planet together, it's nice to pause and reflect once in a while on our shared humanity. Art gives us the opportunity to do that, and I'm so glad Justin shared his art with us.

JULY 2025 LONGLIST

The following list represents the remaining longlisted entries, in no particular order:

- **WILDCARD WINNER** – THE DEAD BIRD by Dinuki Jayawardena
- **WILDCARD WINNER** – WHY DON'T YOU DIE? by Fiona Stoffer
- A LIFE OF ITS OWN by Freya King
- BELTANE by Arabella Peterson
- EVERYWHERE AROUND HERE IS ICE AND COLD by Jornadan Marc
- MIDNIGHT AT THE OASIS by Athena Law
- YOU AND ME VERSUS THE WORLD by Claire Sandys
- HAPPY CAMPERS by Sophie Thompson
- TO HIROSHIMA, WITH LOVE by Sally Reiser Simon
- MY BREASTS by Manu St. Thomas
- REMEMBER SO WE DON'T FORGET by John Scholz

- KNEADED TO DEATH: EPIPHANY IN THE FACE HOLE by Louise Walton
- TINY HOUSES by Christina Wilson
- BUT I DON'T SAY IT by Sarah Kennedy
- SACRAMENT by Zachary Arama
- WHAT CAN BE SAID ABOUT A TRAGEDY? by Madeline Dawn
- HAVE YOU TRIED MANIFESTING SELF-WORTH? by Jack Lewis-Edney
- THE MOLTEN DETRITUS OF A GRIFTER'S PAST by Lincoln Hayes
- A PICTURE THAT WOULD BE PAINTED BY YOU by Michael Stone
- I STILL DON'T LIKE SWIMMING by Kathy Prokhovnik
- DAY by Laura Fulton
- AN OPEN PALM AS A CLENCHED FIST by WM Peregrine
- SOMETIMES A NEST IS JUST FOR A SEASON by Chris Doty-Dunn
- MANGO BUCKETS by Holly Havers
- LIFT TO THE PUB by L. Cook
- IN THE AIR TONIGHT by Holly Sadowski
- BREEDING GROUNDS by Sarah Story
- ROTTEN ONES by Maddie Logemann
- ONE, NOTHING GOES IN THE HOLE, AND TWO, NO ONE GOES IN THE HOLE by Emily Rinkema
- CHANGING FREQUENCIES by Anne Wilkins

- THIS CITADEL HAS BEEN BURNED TO THE GROUND by Linda Atkins
- IT WAS IMPLIED by Corrie Haldane
- THE OVERSEERS by Kennedy Williams
- **DISHONOURABLE MENTION*** – THE POTENTIAL METAPHORICAL AND PHYSICAL CONSEQUENCES OF A SLEEP-DEPRIVED WRITER by Trevor Flanagan

The following story did not make the longlist but received a wildcard prize:

- **WILDCARD WINNER** – GYM SESH by Kerry Goldsworthy

Note: Each judge and assistant judge has awarded a wildcard prize to an entry which did not make the shortlist but which we otherwise felt deserved recognition.

*We sometimes award a cheeky 'Dishonourable mention' to a story which raises our eyebrows in a manner only known to its author.

OCTOBER

2025

Overview

The October 2025 *Not Quite Write Prize for Flash Fiction* challenged writers to create an original piece of fiction of no more than 500 words, which:

included the word **BOOT**.

included the action **'kissing goodbye'**.

broke the writing rule, **'Show, don't tell.'**

The competition drew **344** entries from authors in a reported **16** countries around the world. That's **164,924** words for our judges to read. That's about the same number of words as **_The Grapes of Wrath_** by **John Steinbeck**.

Please enjoy the following top six stories from this round of the competition...

MEN CALLED RUSSELL

W.J. Arthur

The Commodore holds five, but rules be fucked, and we crammed in, all eleven of us, Davo and Russell flat packed into the boot. Dolores sits astride Marty, tulle skirt ruched, as he drives us to Lagoon Dam. I'm squinty eyed with bootleg whisky, pulling party poppers. Their streamers cascade into Dolores' hair and she smiles.

End of exams, end of university, the only enticement before us is the work's treadmill. Marty's ski boat awaits like Cinderella's pumpkin, to force the ball of life to spring. One glorious last chance to make wild memories.

Not one in eleven sober, but Marty knows the route like the veins of his swollen cock, and he drives with fingers gripping Dolores' nipple, tweaking and twisting.

And there she is, the *Devil's Tool*, red paint shimmering in the moonlit water. Marty likes to pay his debts, so Dolores gets first ski, stripping to her bra and panties.

Dolores hangs low, the pale rope limp and sluggish between her legs, the ungainly skis a sinful yellow. Marty opens the throttle, and Dolores lifts like a messiah, a glowing Venus, rising from the waters, one blessed hand erect. Marty turns the boat, sending Dolores swinging across the wake until she loses it, and spins out deep. Dolores' emergency beacons detach, first one ski, then the other.

I pull the rope in, but it is heavier than it should be and I fall back. I've caught a whale, a shark, a fucking $100,000 tuna fish for Japan. The others guffaw, but we spool it in nonetheless, our paycheque for tonight's antics, our just reward.

Dolores is on the end of the line, and we stop for a moment, letting her hang in the water. The rope is around her neck, cutting into her soft flesh. Even in this darkness, I can see the blood. Russell pulls her in, fingers slipping down her wet thighs to bring her on board.

'Holy fuck,' Davo calls before chundering over Dolores, spew slipping into her open mouth, her hair, settling into the corners of her eyes.

I've never respected men called Russell. Russell is the man to watch, the man to fear. You know where you are with a man called Marty. Russell is something else.

Russell leans, checking her pulse, fingers probing the holes in her skin.

'Still alive,' he shouts, clamping his mouth over the spew, sliding a tongue across her face, licking the corners of her mouth. He blows, hooking his pinkie finger under the thin straps of Dolores' bikini.

'Touch her.'

None of us wants to touch those wet and shrivelled paps. A boat full of cowards, we can only think of the spew going down Russell's throat, swirling around in his stomach, and be transfixed by his hands as he caresses Dolores' exposed breasts.

Cowards, one and all.

Marty crams the throttle, and Dolores flips off the back of the boat, legs opening in a flowering cartwheel, rope entwined in her hair like a ribbon.

About the author

W.J. Arthur is determined to become a skilled and prolific writer. To this end, she produces a daily micro fiction. Arthur has just finished her Master of Research in Scottish Folklore and hopes to undertake further ethnographical studies next year. She tries to write happy endings, but sometimes her characters do not oblige.

Author's insights

'I was very driven by the prompts this time, the boot image came quickly, thinking of people in a boot and why they might be there. Initially Russell was going to save Dolores with the kiss goodbye. But characters are wayward and Russell was not what he seemed. Perhaps he sprung from some of the quite awful types who justify their behaviour as just a bit of fun. As a child, my friend got her legs caught in a ski rope and the rope burns were horrific. Once the group were heading to the dam, the story pieces fell together.

'It was my own last week of university for the year, and I was under pressure to get my thesis finished, which made the story darker than I usually write.'

Ed's comments

It's a pity Amanda is no longer doing her swearing stats, because we're closing out 2025 with a bang, or in this case, a 'fuck' (or three!)

Men Called Russell is a dark tale with an even darker ending. We loved the Australianisms and the avoid-cliché-at-all-costs approach to crafting similes. But above all, it was the distinctive narrative voice that got it over the finish line, presenting an unflinching view into the darker side of humanity. The final sentence, rather than offering redemption, causes us to abandon any remaining hope.

Amanda's comments

This story hit like a truck, but left me scratching my head as to how the author had addressed the challenge of this round's anti-prompt, 'Show, don't tell'. In fact, the 'showing' in this story is one of its key strengths. So much so, that it could be the poster child for the concept.

On reflection, I realised the answer lies in one line—central to both the narrative and its theme—which 'tells' the reader how to feel: 'I've never respected men called Russell. Russell is the man to watch, the man to fear. You know where you are with a man called Marty. Russell is something else.'

Truly, the 'bystander effect' is strong in this piece, rendering every member of this party complicit. The perspective character can try all he likes to shift the blame to Russell, but I'm not buying it.

Men Called Russell left me feeling changed, as if I'd been let in on a disturbing secret about humanity. It taught me that, even as late as my forties, it's still possible to lose a little of my innocence.

It's a powerful, provocative, shocking piece of work.

It's art.

0xDEADBEEF

Michael Stone

Sitting on the coffee table, it looked to Nadia more like an oversized, glossy gummy bear with a Teletubby screen. Like a gaudy garden ornament designed by Apple. Or Daft Punk. She wasn't even sure it was on until, with a feeble, electronic voice, it spoke:

«She is angry.»

'Who?' Nadia said. 'Not me, you don't mean?'

«She is angry.»

But she wasn't.

Something's wrong. Nadia unfolded the card-sized owner's manual until it dwarfed her torso. Troubleshooting, troubleshooting. Where's—?

«She is angry.»

'Shush.'

Jesus *Murphy*, why'd they print the text so fine? Right overtop the folds, too.

«She is angry.»

'Shut up,' Nadia snapped. 'That all you say?' Then she laughed at herself, almost sighing. 'If you piss me off, that doesn't really count,' she chided, in that light-hearted, teasing way. The way you might do with—

«She is sad.»

She'd been doing remarkably well, actually, thank you very much. All on her own, too. Without Ms. Pritchard.

That quack. She'd been useless for Nadia's postpartum. That's why Nadia had figured, why not give the AI therapy bot a try? She had the money for one, now.

«She is sad.»

Re-mark-a-bly well. She'd barely been upset pruning Joan Didion from her bookshelves, hadn't she? Had barely been upset when the car seat had peeked into the rearview and startled her.

If anything, wasn't *that* the problem? Nadia was never feeling. Never the right things, anyway. She knew it'd been terrible to feel this way, but when Emily had first arrived— maybe because of the exhaustion—Emily hadn't felt like

Nadia's child at all. Hardly felt like *a* child to begin with. Wasn't Nadia supposed to love her? And she *did*, but—

So why had Emily felt to her more like some machine? Some machine, made of meat. To be upkept, upkept, upkept—

'ERROR,' the bot's screen flashed. '0xDEADBEEF–Invalid Memory.'

Nadia shoved the fucking thing to the floor.

Broken piece of shit.

«She is angry.»

Why hadn't Nadia made Paul turn the fucking car seat around? Just kissed him goodbye, let them drive off?

«She is angry.»

Nadia shot from the couch, kicked the robot, took the phone from its—

Its cradle.

«She is sad.»

No. Nadia had sobbed at the email, when all they'd asked for was his policy number. She wasn't *completely* broken.

Right?

«She is scared.»

'Send someone over here,' Nadia snapped into the phone. 'Fix your goddamn— I tried that! Listen. It needs a reboot, or factory reset, or—'

«I am scared.»

'What'd you say?' Nadia asked. 'Not—not you,' she said, 'shut up,' and smothered the phone into her collar.

'I am scared.'

What'd changed Nadia's feelings for Emily? Her first laugh. First wave goodbye. The time Emily had been propped up in her jumper and a house centipede had scurried by her feet. God, the way she'd looked at Nadia, with her eyes pleading, 'Help me.'

Not 'hungry' or 'thirsty.' Not 'fear.'

'Help *me*.'

Nadia unsmothered the phone. 'Never mind,' she said. 'I—I think I got it working.'

About the author

Michael Stone is a writer living in Ottawa, Canada, whose influences range from Ursula K. Le Guin to Alice Munro, Gabriel Garcia Marquez to Kazuo Ishiguro. His favourite stories are of the weird variety, the ones that blend the speculative and the literary, the ones that are surreal or strange or off kilter. Also, stories that make him cry. Preferably, they're weird and make him cry. One day he hopes to complete a novel that'll fit that bill, but in the meantime, flash and short fiction are keeping him occupied.

Author's insights

'In programming, there's a way of representing binary in what's called a hexadecimal number, and they're typically prefixed with "0x" to indicate them as being such. Basically, each "digit" can represent one of sixteen values, using the letters A-F for 10-15. If you've ever used Photoshop or MS Paint and seen those codes for the colour picker, that's hexadecimal.

'Programmers liked to use those hexadecimal numbers to spell things out for error codes so they're recognizable, I suppose, and 0xDEADBEEF is one of them. I don't remember when I'd come across this particular one, but it struck me. It was so strange and a little morbid, and it got stuck in my mind. 0xDEADBEEF has existed in my notes app for a while now as a possible story kernel, but never in the form of my *Not Quite Write Prize* submission. I always imagined like, hey, if I ever have a robot assassin character or something, DEADBEEF would be a pretty cool name for that.

'Once I saw the 'boot' prompt, and my mind went to 'reboot', that's when I remembered that 0xDEADBEEF idea. But I dropped the robot assassin idea fairly quickly. I was thinking about a chart I saw which showed what AI is used for the most, and how that's changed since its early days. I was surprised to see that, nowadays, "therapy/companionship" was the number two use. That inspired me in a couple ways. One was the idea that a good way to do telling while still having it be interesting or engaging would be if an AI therapist were to say explicitly what a character's emotions are, but for that character to betray those emotions somehow.

'But I think the bigger inspiration was understanding why someone might use AI therapy in the first place. As I said, AI as therapy being the number two most popular use really surprised me. As someone fortunate enough not to have needed therapy, I didn't really get it. I'd have imagined the human element would be important for something like therapy. But then again, I know people who've gone to therapy, and when they haven't clicked with the therapist, they've described it to me like the person they were talking to didn't really understand them. Like they were just reciting lines and mantras and exercises that they'd read somewhere else. Like an AI spitting out training data.

'And I wanted to approach that topic of AI therapy. Not in a judgmental way, I hoped, but in a way to understand. Throughout the writing of this story, I started asking myself questions I hadn't really thought about before. Like, how much do we project our own meaning onto the things we experience? The things we see and hear? Can it really be therapy when a human pours their heart into a machine, and that lifeless, mindless machine pumps it through a series of calculations to spit out an output? And if that works for someone, does it really matter?

'*0xDEADBEEF* was the result of trying to tie all these disparate ideas together into something coherent.'

Ed's comments

I love how this story is constructed: the way the 'faulty' therapy bot forces Nadia to work though her issues, and the way her past is revealed to us progressively through their interaction, not to mention the devastating way the word 'cradle' instantly flips her emotional state.

The 0XDEADBEEF error was new to me, but it's such a compelling motif around which to gather these themes of loss and blame, and the interface between human and machine, becoming more a part of our lives every day.

Amanda's comments

As readers, whether consciously or otherwise, we become most frustrated with 'telling' when an author tells us how to *feel* instead of trusting us to reach reasonable conclusions on our own. In this story, Michael takes that idea to its extreme, inventing a therapy bot whose sole function is... exactly that.

Not being an IT expert, I had to look up the 0XDEADBEEF error. I'm still not entirely sure what it means, but what fascinates me is that my empathy for this fictional character seems to transcend that lack of understanding. Some experiences, like infant and partner loss, just cannot 'compute'. They require something more of us—something deeper than logic.

And that, for now, is what separates us from the machines.

THE WAY OUT

Steven Huff

Then there was the year of the shed-pocalypse—when all the men went into their sheds.

That makes it sound global, but as far as we know, it was confined to an L-shaped block of Spearwood, off Ukich Crescent. Yugoslavia had been all over the news that summer—ethnic cleansing, camps, Milošević—and, later, learning the absent men had all been Croats, people would nod knowingly. But Dad'd been four when Deda and Baba emigrated, and if he shouted any louder at the airstrikes than at the football, or Johnny Howard's GST, us kids didn't notice.

We didn't even have a shed, so it started with us fighting over ride-alongs on endless Bunnings trips. Then the great novelty of construction—Dad mopping his bald spot with his T-shirt, rehydrating with Emu Export, swatting stray offspring—ending, for us, when the Colorbond walls went up, and Dad dragged in the remaining materials, his swag, their bedroom TV, and, with a peck Mum didn't register as a goodbye, disappeared.

Mum'd just had Liza, her sixth, and her initial reaction was a tired shrug. If Dad wanted to yell at Champion's League in the early hours, she'd rather he was in the shed—as for the rest, the last thing she needed was a seventh. So she started sending us out with trays, and leaving the laundry unlocked for him to use the dunny. He still left early for the warehouse, coming back grease-stained and knackered, until he just stopped, and work gave him the boot.

It wasn't just him. All over, you could hear women shouting, pleading, banging shed doors. Soon, they started coming around, bringing or receiving pots of food, minding each other's children. They said Mrs. Vlahov tried to starve her man out, but panicked and gave in after two weeks. For months, we heard drilling, grinding, hammering. Mum put a cardboard sign on Dad's ute, and three days later the ute was gone. We had Weet-Bix for dinner more often.

One evening, when I'd been shooed out for overhearing Mum say it was about time to run a good long spin cycle, I found the shed door ajar.

Once my eyes adjusted, I saw Dad in the middle, kneeling in front of what seemed to be an empty doorframe. He had hold of something down at the base of the frame—something slippery, the way he was struggling and cursing—and was peeling it up, letting golden light spill out beneath.

I must've gasped, because he flinched, losing his grip, and whatever he'd been *opening* slammed shut, leaving nothing but an unpainted doorframe.

Other abandoned frames, in various shapes, loomed in the dark.

I froze, expecting to cop it good, but when he turned, tears were running into his moustache.

Over the following days, they all came out—thin, corpse-pale, unshaven—and moved back into their houses and their wives' beds, and went on with their lives. All except Dan Sumich, who was never seen again, and who everyone said must've run away to Broome.

But I knew better.

About the author

Steve lives in Perth, where he buys books at a faster rate than he reads them, provides domestic services to two cats, and writes when given a deadline.

Author's insights

'This one started with the original version of the opening line popping into my head: "Then there was the year all the men went into their sheds." I had no idea where it was going, but it felt like something. I decided, with three Australian judges, that I didn't need to hold back on the Aussie references (apologies to international readers not acquainted with the pleasures of Emu Export or childhood trips to Bunnings). And with an opening line like that, and because I like weird fiction, it had to take a turn for the weird.'

Ed's comments

The Way Out feels inspired by real events. The setting is a real place, as is its ethnic makeup. Yet, what follows is highly surreal. Steven never 'shows' us exactly what mysterious, slippery secrets the dads are hiding, but we can recognise their parallels in the real world. Perhaps they are looking for space away from their young families, or perhaps they are searching for home—whatever that might mean to an immigrant who doesn't entirely belong in either country.

Amanda's comments

This is one of those stories that gets under your skin. What does it *mean?* But perhaps a more important question is, what does it *mean* to *you?*

For me, this story was an exploration of what some describe as the male suicide epidemic and the quiet withdrawal that too often precedes tragedy. For me, those empty doorframes—a metaphor for escape—conjured images of hanging bodies. For me, the tears in the moustache resonated in a silent cry for help.

When blindly judging this story, I had no way of knowing Steven's authorial intention. Did he really mean all that, or was I projecting my own fears onto something much lighter? Left alone with my thoughts, I worried deeply for Dan Sumich.

As I read Steven's words back now, I'm given pause to reflect on the beauty of human connection through art. I'm also sadly reminded of the simpler connection that eludes so many of us in our contemporary world.

In Australia each year, we celebrate R U OK DAY? It's a day dedicated to suicide prevention and mental health awareness, which encourages us to check in with friends, family, and colleagues by asking the simple question, 'Are you okay?'

As I now connect with *you*, the reader of this book, through my own words, I just want to say, 'I hope you're okay. But if you're not, for whatever reason, I know enough about this crazy world to promise you it *will* get better... You just need to open the right door.'

STEP RIGHT UP

Dawn Goulet

Hell is what we called her. Heloise Anne-Laure Lefèvre. Helly with the greenest eyes and the blackest hair. Helly with lips like cherries. She joined us in Baton Rouge but always swore she was born in Paris. I, for one, believed her.

We had an old carnie named Claude, a master with chisel or saw, and he made the whole thing, to her precise specifications: the raised platform, the stool, and KISSING BOOTH spelled out in red and gold, but with the 'H' always coming loose, swinging down from its nail. A ghost, Helly said. I didn't go in for such things, to be honest, but I'd have believed the sky was green if Helly told me it was so.

Ah, you've found my initials there. Don't look surprised. A tattooed man can draw on more than flesh! Those were the posters that brought the crowds. My bearded lady, my flying trapeze, my lion tamer with the thrashing whip. KISSING

BOOTH! Helly's said. 5¢ Smooches. Pucker up for a real French kiss!

You should have seen her work a crowd. Winking and pouting, flouncing her skirts. The whistles when she pushed a man down onto her stool, when she tied the red silk scarf across his eyes. He was not likely to get a kiss from our Helly, though, was he? And he knew it, smiling as the crowd jeered. She'd pass a rosebud across his lips, or a finger dipped in chocolate. She'd hold her little dog up for a lick or let Rosie the elephant prod him with her quivering trunk. The crowd roared, the scarf was lifted, and the man sallied forth, to be slapped on the back and bought drinks.

Why suffer such indignities? Why pay for it? Only this. One in a hundred—two hundred? five?—received a proper kiss from our Helly. A kiss that took a man's breath away, that set the crowd afire, that lingered long, until all was quiet, save the lone whistle of an old-timer, the better part of a century under his belt, who had, for all he'd seen in this world, never, never, been kissed like that. The line for Helly's booth wound round the midway.

But all things end, don't they? There was a contest. A soda company needed a new logo, and I gave them a scroll of white letters against a field of red. They asked me to come draw for them, if you can believe it. Beach beauties, jolly Santas, flush-faced lads on bikes, all tipping back dewy bottles of their soda pop. And so, I took leave of the circus.

As I left my tent in the half-lit dawn, Helly stepped from the shadows and took my arm. She never minded the pictures there, you know. She traced them with her fingers. Step right up, friend, she said, and sat me down on her stool.

What do you think? Was I one in a hundred? Two hundred? Five?

Wouldn't you like to know.

About the author

Dawn is a Chicago-area writer who drafts legal opinions by day and fiction in all the moments in between making soup, observing rabbits, going on adventures with her family, and taking Jim the Dog for suburban sniffaris. She loves a good prompt and a deadline!

Author's insights

'This is my first ever *Not Quite Write* story. A friend encouraged me to join her in the competition, and I loved it! The "kiss goodbye" and "boot" prompts immediately made me think of a kissing booth, and the "show, don't tell" anti-prompt had me searching for a narrator with a unique voice.

'There is an apocryphal story in my family that a great-great-uncle was the tattooed man in a circus and won a contest to design the new logo for a certain famous carbonated beverage. I have found absolutely no evidence that any part of that story is true (and I've looked, because wouldn't that be amazing?), but of all the characters, real or imagined, who I would love to have tell me a story, he is certainly one.'

Ed's comments

This piece is all about character: the mysterious and captivating Helly. I love the way Dawn establishes her historical setting through detail alone, without ever having to explicitly tell us. She paints Helly vividly through the eyes of her narrator but reveals very little about the narrator himself. We never even learn his name. But then, he's not the star of the show...

Amanda's comments

Dawn offers such a playful interpretation of the anti-prompt here, twisting 'Kiss and tell' into 'Kiss and don't show,' that I couldn't help but succumb to the story's many charms.

As the only 'light' story in the 'shade' of this particular shortlist, it reads like a breath of fresh air. I adored its rich, scene-setting details, and the time-period-perfected narrative voice, which together lend the story a feel reminiscent of Tim Burton's *Big Fish*.

As a huge fan of the 'scroll of white letters against a field of red,' I feel compelled to state in writing that this is *not* the true origin story of that iconic logo. But does it really matter? This detail so perfectly encapsulates the time period (without the need to 'tell' us what it is) that it feels right at home.

I confess, I would gladly sit through any number of this narrator's tall tales and never question another thing.

THE GRIEF

Chloe Paige

Once again, I lie underneath my parents' backyard gumtree, my mouth parched shut from The Grief.

The tree's papery branches reach for the cloudy grey the way I reached, splay-fingered for Mum. The rusty clothesline squeaks—the same Hills Hoist I swung on in '96 when Tully's water restrictions ended. Dad sprayed the hose just 'cause he could, laughing, *'Now this is living, Josh! Drink it in while it lasts!'*

It didn't last. The Grief's made a new drought inside me.

But there's gotta be something to drink somewhere else. I stand, staggering away from the house I inherited. Past the corner milk bar, past the playground, and to the airport, leaving Tully behind.

When the plane coughs me out into dusty orange Meekatharra, The Grief follows me here. Course it bloody does.

My lips shrivel into a scowl. I shuffle into a muggy coffeeshop with a ceiling fan thwapping around grit. The redheaded, pierced-lip barista leans forward, all smiles and drink-me-in cleavage. If I could, I'd scrape my swollen, throbbing tongue over her piercing. Kiss her mouth open. Steal her saliva.

She offers me her phone number, but I'm staring at the steaming mug she clinks onto a saucer. It's coffee. *Not Tully-milk-bar coffee.* I smash it on the floor and piss off back to the airport.

A day spent bumbling around Alice Springs, then I cuff a tourist for climbing Uluru like how I climbed Tully's playground.

A month in Kalgoorlie. The Grief cracks my mouth's film of dried sweat because I saw a bushfire-bitten gum leaf shaped like Tully's golden gumboot monument.

A year in Yulara and two in Oodnadatta and three or thirty in Coober Pedy and lost count at Lyndhurst and *fuck this.*

Fuck losing myself in the spinifex. Home's *Tully.* Soggy verandas and backyard hoses. People I never wanted to say goodbye to.

So, I fly home. Rumbling thunderclouds blacken Tully as I stagger through humid streets, past The Golden Gumboot, and freeze.

The playground's gone.

The milk bar's a Woolies.

No. I puppeteer my creaky limbs to my parents' house. In the window, a wide-eyed, cobweb-trapped reflection stares back.

It's *me*, all grey hair and saggy jowls. The Grief salts my throat—I lived a whole life without drinking it in. I never smelled the coffee or listened to Dreamtime stories. I never knew The Joy from chatting to tourists or The Love from marrying a smiling redhead or The Bliss from reading our kids *Possum Magic* while rain splattered the roof. All because I let The Grief evaporate me, and now I'm dying of thirst.

I step away from the window. With The Resignation, I head to the backyard.

Once again, I lie underneath my parents' gumtree, admiring the green rustling leaves swaying against the glorious raincloud bloom above until I can't anymore. Until my ribs stick up from the ground like white saplings; until rain falls and kisses me goodbye; until The Grief decays with me, and my mouth opens, drinking from the sky.

About the author

Chloe writes on the salty shores of Wadawurrung Country in Geelong, Australia. She is published in a tiny handful of lit mags, but her favourite is this one. Chloe adores strong verbs, bastardising grammar, and rambling about poetic devices to people who truly couldn't care less.

Chloe's work features twice in this anthology. You can find her other contribution on page 79.

Author's insights

'Writing this story coincided with the 40th anniversary of the Australian Government returning rightful ownership of Uluru to the Anangu Aboriginal people. With that, it felt timely to write an Aussie story about coming home.

'Often my flash stories involve me practicing a new style or technique. This time I was toying with how sounds can affect pacing. For example, the "A year in Yulara" line blends similar sounds together to help speed things up, like time flying by. Plosives (heavy sounds: p, b, t, d, k, g) are clumped together in places to slow the reader down and focus on some extra important bits. All of this means I fretted over every single word choice, which was my own damn fault. I still needed to make these words suit the vibe because all the while I kept hearing Amanda's voice in my head, whisper-yelling: *Single Effect! Poe's Single Effect!*'

Ed's comments

The imagery of The Grief mirrors that of Australia itself: dry and unforgiving. It's a warning. An ode to nostalgia, to loss, and a lament that one can never truly return home. That nothing in the world remains the same forever, and that we must change with it, or be forced to languish in regret.

The closing image is devastating and poignant. The weight of realisation hits hard, yet it offers the hope of a new beginning.

Amanda's comments

In response to the anti-prompt, Chloe has turned the advice 'Never name an emotion' on its head, elevating The Grief, The Joy, The Love, The Bliss and The Resignation to proper noun status.

This is a story where 'Poe's Single Effect' shines: every detail points towards a single emotional impact—this experience of grief as a kind of drying out. I found the imagery of 'ribs stick(ing) up from the ground like white saplings' to be particularly evocative, but the prose itself feels arid and brittle, mirroring the emotion Chloe conveys.

Although it's steeped in missed opportunities and lifelong regret, I also see it as story of hope. In Australia, we know all too well that, while the droughts may be harsh, the flooding rains *will* come again.

THE GHOSTS YOU BRING WITH YOU

Chris Doty-Dunn

You decided to move into this house even after reading the disclosures. Maybe you don't believe in ghosts. Maybe you made the same joke I did, about a pair of spectral hands to help a single mom with chores.

Regardless, if you're holding this letter, you're also holding the keys. So.

Your new home is not haunted.

Mrs. Philips lives next door. She'll bring peach cobbler and peer around you into the foyer, asking if you know what happened here. If you've seen or heard strange things. Don't let her scare you. Just say you don't believe in all that and that you'll return the dish soon, thanks for the welcome.

You'll hear footsteps in the attic late at night, my father's boots when he'd come home reeking of whiskey and rage. They might sound different to you—like whatever scares you the most. But it's just wind through the rafters.

Eyes will peer in through the windows at the full moon. They looked bleary and bloodshot to me, but Jenny saw that bully, Nancy Elliot. No matter whose faces they wear, know that it's possums or raccoons, nothing more.

Draw the blinds.

Go to bed.

The lights will turn off and on by themselves—old wiring is all. There's no pattern in the flashes. No messages in Morse code from long-dead grandmothers who were the only refuge from the fighting.

You won't want to hear the things they have her say, anyway.

The doors will get stuck. Old houses settle. If you find yourself trapped, close your eyes and pretend you've locked yourself in a closet until the screaming stops. When it's quiet and you come out, at least Mom won't be crying on the couch, holding a bag of ice against her eye.

The most important rule, though, as important as remembering that the house is not haunted, is this. If your loved ones are scared, don't leave them alone. Don't give Jenny a peck on the cheek and run off to work like I did.

You have to stay until her terror subsides with the rising sun.

Because the things that live in this house will feed on your fear. Twist it and point it back at you. Don't let them know you've seen or heard them. Don't scream, and don't run. Because every reaction wears you down until...

It's too late for me.

I thought I'd lost my mind, that Dad had clawed out of his grave to follow us. But the only ghosts here are the ones you've brought with you, and they'd follow you anywhere.

Now you have rational explanations. There's no reason to be afraid. No matter what you see or hear.

I hope this letter helps you.

You probably won't see her—she's my fear, not yours—but if you catch a glimpse of an eleven-year-old girl with pigtails and a red dress hanging in the upstairs closet...

Tell her Mommy's so sorry for not believing how scared she was of Nancy.

About the author

Chris Doty-Dunn mostly writes weird, speculative fiction, often with a queer bent. He holds a PhD in linguistics and aspires to learn all the languages. A certified contest goblin, he lives outside Boston, Massachusetts with his husband and their two dogs, Weland and Waffles.

Read more at chrisdotydunn.com.

Author's insights

'The *Not Quite Write* anti-prompt always twists my brain into knots trying to come up with a unique take. To my mind, "showing" is a way of asking the reader to infer based on character behavior—emotional state, dishonesty, whatever. That's preferred to telling, in part, because it invites the reader in and makes them a part of what's unfolding. In this piece, I tried to take "telling" very literally, while still asking that the reader come into the house and peek around the corners (and maybe catch a glimpse of something they shouldn't while they're there).'

Ed's comments

As someone who doesn't believe in ghosts, I rarely find ghost stories particularly scary. People, on the other hand, can be spooky as hell. The events hinted at in this epistolary story send a chill down my spine precisely for that reason. Because though ghosts are not real, our deepest fears can be.

And they don't disappear when you turn on the light.

Amanda's comments

There's something heartbreaking about this line: 'The only ghosts here are the ones you've brought with you, and they'd follow you anywhere.' It lands like a gut punch, demanding self-reflection.

I love when a story can do that—pull us out of ourselves and into the page. It feels like an invitation to join in the meaning-making, to carry the story forward in our own minds and follow it down our own path.

We all know what it is to be afraid, and we all know what it means to haul emotional baggage through life. What Chris captures so effectively here is that universal fear of being unable to outrun our inner demons, and of accepting them (whether we want to or not) as an inextricable part of who we are.

OCTOBER 2025 LONGLIST

The following list represents the remaining longlisted entries, in no particular order:

- **WILDCARD WINNER** – MY BROTHER by Lucy Mac
- **WILDCARD WINNER** – GUIDED RELAXATION by Ellen-Arwen Tristram
- UPPING THE ANTE by Brandon Woo
- ST KARMA'S FETE: COME FOR THE PATTY-PAN TOFFEES, STAY FOR THE RECKONING by Romany Jane
- AN ARCHAIC AND BRUTAL WORD by Taurenelle
- IN THE ENGLISH WAY by R.C. Barajas
- EVERY MORNING WE KISS GOODNIGHT by T.J. Burgoyne
- THINGS I DON'T TELL YOU IN THE QUEUE AT CHIPOTLE by Ben Daggers
- DOWNWARD-FACING DOUG by Chad Frame
- MOMMY, KISS ME GOODBYE by Lida Kanari

- DEMONSLAND by John Scholz
- THE IRONY OF A MALADAPTIVE MIND by N. M. Fadzli
- HER GREATEST ASSET by Rananda | The Ink Rat
- WHEN I WAS TWELVE by Skye Moor
- MOONSHINE SPEAKS EASY by Janelle Grenon
- A BLUSH MOON RISING OVER THE MOUNTAINS OF AIDA by Lorena Otes
- BASTARD KEYS by Sam James
- KNOBBY AND THE JON by Hideo Kuahiwi
- HOW DO YOU FEEL TODAY? by Melissa Jornd
- REIGNITION by Jaden Christopher
- TELL ME WHAT THE WORLD LOOKS LIKE by Josh Lowe
- NIKO'S LIGHT by Roger Vickery
- B LINE — 'EXPRESS TO WARD ON THE AVE.' by Lily Finch
- JUST SAY IT by Angella Hayes
- LIGHTS, CAMERA, SILENCE by Marissa Hanley
- MONOTONY by Deidra Whitt Lovegren
- A CONFESSIONAL by Exeter T. Stevens
- A REALLY BIG SHEW (AS ED SULLIVAN WOULD SAY) by Edgar J. Lavoie
- I NEED THIS LIKE I NEED A HEAD IN THE HOLE. by Sarah Kennedy
- FOR KEVIN'S SAKE by Emily Rinkema
- DELUSIONS by Philippa Freegard
- TRICHOTILLOMANIAC by Kelli Johnson
- THE CLICKER by Heather Pownall

- **DISHONOURABLE MENTION*** – THE FAIRY GODMOTHER'S MONOLOGUE (TO BE PERFORMED ALONE ON STAGE, DIRECTLY ADDRESSING THE AUDIENCE) by Caro Robson

The following story did not make the longlist but received a wildcard prize:

- **WILDCARD WINNER** – THE LITTLE MUG WITH THE CHRISTMAS PUDDING by Hope Walker

Note: Each judge and assistant judge has awarded a wildcard prize to an entry which did not make the shortlist but which we otherwise felt deserved recognition.

*We sometimes award a cheeky 'Dishonourable mention' to a story which raises our eyebrows in a manner only known to its author.

Acknowledgements

A round of applause to the authors whose prize-winning work features in this book: Taurenelle, W.J. Arthur, Alexandria Bellani, Isabelle Berns, Jo Binns, Holly Brandon, Alisa Coddington, Justin Creps, Chris Doty-Dunn, Dawn Goulet, E. C. Heath, Steven Huff, Sam James, Ella Micallef, Elda Orozco, Chloe Paige, Greg Schmidt, Kris Schnebelen, Elise Scott, Malte Springer, Michael Stone, and Louise Walton. Your stories have left an indelible mark not only on these pages, but on our hearts. We can't wait to see where your talents take you next!

A special thanks to Dean Koorey, who this year agreed to hang up his Uniball Jetstream 1.0 and join the *Not Quite Write* team as a lowly 'assistant' judge (despite possessing infinitely more flash fiction judging experience than Ed and Amanda put together).

A *huge* thanks to our spouses, 'Shadow' Sharon and 'Arson' Andy, and our daughters, Tara and Carissa, and Isla and Skye, for being the rootinest tootinest band of outlaws this side of

Death Valley, and for supporting *Not Quite Write* to thrive. We remain eternally grateful for your patience and support.

Amanda would like to extend her personal thanks to Bronwyn Lohan (a.k.a. Mum) for gifting her with a love of words and a loud mouth (but also for not dying back in March despite giving it a red-hot go—there's only so much drama a girl can handle...)

Thanks also to The Coven: Jayne Rice, Jess Popplewell, Jo Lyons, Julia Boggio, Farrah Riaz, and Cristal Phillips for your whole-hearted support and enthusiasm (and for not kicking Amanda out of the gang, despite the fact that she rarely writes these days).

To our fellow Coasties, including the team behind Words on the Waves, the CoastWrite crew, Rabs from the Podvan podcast, as well as local booksellers, Book Face Erina and the Umina Beach Book Nook, thanks for playing your part in our vibrant local writing community, and for helping to spread the word about *Not Quite Write*.

To the people who made us look good this year: Vanessa Browne (cover design), Kendell Marjanovic (photography), and of course our 2025 Artist-in-Residence, Camsyn Clair (whose artwork features throughout this anthology), thank you.

A massive shoutout to our brave 2025 Daredevils: Linda Atkins, Alexandria Bellani, S.A. Braden, Natalie Bucsko, Eilish Forwells, Stephanie Hewat Simmonds, Sarah Kennedy, Justin Kramasz, Marina R. M. Lane, Jennifer Lyons-Bell, MJ McElhaney, Mohnam/Kurosh, Pennie Nichols, Holly

Sadowski, S J Snyder, Exeter Stevens, Alyson Tait, and Dez Veares. Thank you for trusting us with your egos. The *Not Quite Write Prize* and *Podcast* would not be the same without you and your unforgettable stories.

Finally, a huge thank you to ALL our *Not Quite Write Prize* entrants. You continue to amaze us with your boundless creativity and your willingness to put it all on the line, every single time. It is our great joy and privilege to bring this competition to you, and to play some small part in your writing journeys.

With all of your continued support, we feel confident to say the biggest things are yet to come. We can't wait to embark on a brand-new adventure with you all in 2026.

Inspired by these stories?

Why not enter the next round of the
Not Quite Write Prize for Flash Fiction?

notquitewriteprize.com

Praise for the *Not Quite Write Prize*

'Just love what you guys do—the pod, the comp, and the fact that you clearly both want the best for everyone who enters. Not everyone is so encouraging in their feedback. While you guys are honest in your critiques on the podcast, there's always a sense that you really want the best for each contestant.'

— Sarah Kennedy

'This was my first time doing *Not Quite Write* and it was really fun! I was baffled by the anti-prompt, but in a good way. I like my final story, and I rejected some other ideas that I might turn into stories later. I'll be back!'

— Jessica Sedgewick

'My son and I both signed up, and it was fun seeing how differently we used the prompts.'

— Sandra Thom-Jones

'This is my first time entering a *Not Quite Write* competition. I have given myself the goal of experimenting with my writing more this year. This certainly helped to challenge me and to get my creative juices flowing. With the time limit, it enabled me to not overthink, but to write from the soul.'

— Grace Dove

'For my money, this is the best contest going. Thanks for all you do to make it so.'

— Thom Brodkin

Connect with us

The *Not Quite Write Podcast* is available on all major podcasting platforms. Search for us on your platform of choice or scan the QR code below.

notquitewrite.com

Connect with us on social media

 @notquitewrite.com

 @NQWpodcast

 @NotQuiteWritePodcast

 @NotQuiteWritePodcast

PO Box 9067
Wyoming NSW
AUSTRALIA 2250

contact@notquitewrite.com

We value your support

All books live or die on the recommendations of their readers. If you enjoyed this book, please spread the word!

You can support this book and its authors by:

- Buying a copy for yourself and/or loved ones
- Encouraging other people to buy a copy
- Rating and reviewing the book online
- Sharing a review on social media
- Talking about the book with other readers
- Liking and sharing *Not Quite Write* social media posts
- Engaging in performative reading of the book in high-traffic public spaces

Thank you for all you do to support
the creative arts and artists.

Other books by Not Quite Write

Best of the Not Quite Write Prize for Flash Fiction 2023-2024

Marvel as our authors embrace adverbs and clichés, eschew dialogue tags, pump out purple prose, and head-hop their way to a series of colourful, beautiful, and sometimes disturbing pieces. Enjoy author insights and inspiration plus commentary from the *Not Quite Write* judges, and wave goodbye to any limits you thought existed in the world of flash fiction.

AVAILABLE NOW FROM AMAZON & NOTQUITEWRITE.COM

'Coming' soon...

FLESH Fiction Collection

In 2025, the *Not Quite Write Prize for FLESH Fiction* enticed authors aged 18+ from around the world to craft erotic short stories inspired by the theme, *'Making the unsexy irresistible.'*

Join us in 2026 for the release of the collected best of the best. Whether you prefer slow-burn seductions or deliciously depraved delights, inanimate object romance, monster sex or just plain old human intimacy, we're thrilled to bring you a curated collection of the most captivating, clever, and downright tempting pieces.

Prepare to challenge what you find *irresistible*.

HITTING AMAZON & NOTQUITEWRITE.COM IN 2026

www.ingramcontent.com/pod-product-compliance
Lightning Source LLC
Chambersburg PA
CBHW011558190726
48287CB00010B/2958